Graffiti on wall in Old City of Jerusalem

Published by Bourne to Write

Copyright © 2023 Lesley Dawson

ISBN: 9798395474995

Front cover: Louis Frost from an original
painting by Lesley Dawson

How Far Is It To Bethlehem?

Memories & Stories

Lesley Dawson

CONTENTS

Acknowledgments   i

1   Confrontation   Pg 3

2   Left Behind   Pg 5

3   From the Beginning, it Went Wrong   Pg 7

4   It isn't What I Expected   Pg 9

5   Upside Down   Pg 11

6   A Sign of the Times   Pg 14

7   The Value of Friendship   Pg 16

8   None of Them Knew the Colour of the Sky   Pg 18

9   I Had a Dream   Pg 20

10   This Christmas was Going to be Different   Pg 22

11   Would She Come Again?   Pg 24

12   Jaffa Oranges   Pg 26

13   I Want to do Something Improbable   Pg 28

14   Rent a Family   Pg 30

15   People who Travel are Always Fugitives   Pg 32

16   The People Upstairs   Pg 34

17   The House is Silent Now   Pg 36

18   Too Many Visitors?   Pg 38

How far is it to Bethlehem?

19	Where am I?	Pg 40
20	The Sweetest Taste	Pg 43
21	A Christmas Event	Pg 44
22	Sister Susan	Pg 46
23	Lateral Thinking	Pg 48
24	Friends Across the Line	Pg 49
25	The Retreat	Pg 52
26	It was Love at First Sight	Pg 63
27	Shalom	Pg 65
28	Taxi	Pg 76
29	The Weekend we all Became Spanish	Pg 69
30	Some People Say	Pg 71
31	Leaving Gaza	Pg 73
32	The Curfew	Pg 75
33	Something I had been Meaning to tell You	Pg 77
34	Party Pooper	Pg 79
35	Sisters	Pg 81
36	The Year Without a Summer	Pg 83
37	Ten Days Under Fire	Pg 86
38	Waiting for Saddam	Pg 88
39	Pray for the Priests of Jerusalem	Pg 90

40	Is it Necessary?	Pg 92
41	I Remember, I Remember	Pg 95
42	There Are Never Really Endings	Pg 97
43	Graduation	Pg 99
44	You See But You Don't Observe	Pg 102
45	The Deadline	Pg 104
46	You Think it will Never Happen	Pg 106
47	Friends or Enemies?	Pg 108
48	Afternoon Tea with a Difference	Pg 111
49	An Inherited Trait	Pg 113
50	House to Let	Pg 115
51	At the Hairdressers	Pg 128
52	A Very Special Woman	Pg 130
53	So Much Depends Upon	Pg 132
54	Just Smile	Pg 134
55	Living the Dream	Pg 136
56	Student Strike	Pg 138
57	Wait	Pg 140
58	Panic	Pg 142
59	A Dangerous Monster	Pg 144
60	A Brief History of Betrayal	Pg 147

61	A Most Unusual Angel	Pg 149
62	How Does it Feel to be Followed	Pg 152
63	Not What I Wanted At All	Pg 154
64	Who Has the Last Word?	Pg 156
65	Bit of a Bombshell part 1 & 2	Pg 158
66	Feeling at Home	Pg 162
67	Great Expectations	Pg 164
68	Forgive Me	Pg 166
69	Coming Home?	Pg 168
70	Nostalgia	Pg 170
71	The Dream	Pg 172
72	We Said We Wouldn't Look Back	Pg 174
73	Poem to my Students	Pg 177
74	The Siege of Bethlehem	Pg 178
75	Another Manic Monday	Pg 180
76	Being Interviewed	Pg 183
	Photographs	Pg 185

How far is it to Bethlehem?

To Roddy, my Creative Writing Workshop (CWW) tutor who helped me to see that I could write and to my fellow CWW members for encouraging me to write these stories. Many thanks to Louis Frost for the book cover design.

To friends, colleagues and students who shared many of these adventures, on both sides of the Green Line. I am grateful for all you taught me.

Writing as a Brit I am sure that I may have misunderstood some of the cultural issues involved and I ask for forgiveness where this is true. All mistakes are mine alone.

The proceeds from this book are being donated to an organization working with people with disability, Action around Bethlehem Children with Disability (ABCD).

Confrontation

Eight o'clock in the morning is not the best time to be facing hostile security guards after an overnight flight from London to Tel Aviv. Any time of the day or night it is not pleasant to be faced with Israeli security, especially when you are about to start a new job working at Bethlehem University in the West Bank and you can't answer their questions about where you will be staying. I had packed my bags, having received an excess baggage allowance from Save the Children Fund for my British Airways flight two days before and had headed to London to stay with friends who were even more surprised than myself about where I was going.

By now I was used to the jokes; "I hope you have a tin helmet!"

"Have you got a flak jacket?"

"Can you zig and zag?" and "Don't let anyone gallop off into the desert with you on a camel, unless they give you your weight in emeralds."

This was 1988 in the middle of the First Intifada, the Palestinian uprising against Israeli occupation, September first to be precise, and I was about to experience my first semester teaching Palestinian Arab students.

But before all this I had to get through Israeli security. I stood in line in front of a booth labelled 'Foreign Passports' and waited to meet my fate.

When my turn came, I faced the neutral, bored eyes of a young Israeli woman dressed in military uniform, whose badge named her as Rachel.

I watched those eyes turn from neutral and bored to hostile and wide awake when I admitted that I was going to Bethlehem in the West Bank.

She wanted to know where I would be working, and I couldn't say because all Palestinian universities had been closed by military order. She wanted to know where I would be living, and I didn't know because nobody at the university had given me an address and most expats get their post from PO Boxes as not many West Bank streets have names. She wanted to know what I would be doing, and I could answer this question and said I would be teaching physiotherapy to Palestinian students.

At this point her hostility turned to scepticism as she asked, "do the Arabs know what physiotherapy is?" I assured her that they did, and she shrugged her shoulders disdainfully. However, she did stamp my passport with a visa for 3 months, so I heaved a sigh of relief and thanked her. She wished me good luck in a tone of voice that implied that I was going to need it.

I was given a small blue ticket that allowed me finally to enter the Baggage Reclaim where I started to gather up my six suitcases. After all I was going to stay in Bethlehem for four years and a girl needs her things around her to make life bearable.

Left Behind

There it was sitting on the edge of the baggage carousel, waiting to be discovered. I held my breath and waited for the storm to come. Everybody else collected their cases and strolled off to the 'Nothing to Declare' exit.

Then it happened. Bustling across came a porter with a walkie talkie. He looked around and asked a few people if the box belonged to them. All shook their heads and hurried out, worried what might be in the box. My porter friend spoke urgently into his receiver and within seconds the area was flooded with security men and women, all of whom had unclipped their weapons. This crowd of young fit, hard, unsmiling people gathered round the box at a safe distance and seemed unsure of what to do next. Not knowing what to do didn't impair their voices and the level of noise rose as they became more and more agitated, in very loud explosive Hebrew.

By now all arriving passengers had been cleared away from the potential bomb and the carousel had been stopped with half a plane load of luggage stuck on top of the carousel lift and the other half stuck in the bowels of the baggage tunnel.

The sirens were now going and there was the sound of passengers rushing out of the building. Enter Mr. Big. Big in size and obviously big in influence. He brought with him a bomb disposal team all clothed in heavy clothes and wearing helmets with masks. They certainly looked the part.

A very long pair of tong-like metal pieces were waved in the direction of the box until they caught hold of the flaps on the top of the box and it began to open. There was now no sound as we waited for the explosion and expected the bomb disposal people to blow it up. When nothing happened, one of the more adventurous guys was prodded by Mr. Big to move closer.

When he investigated the box, he laughed out loud and beckoned his colleagues to join him.

Eventually we all saw the contents a huge chocolate birthday cake.

As one of the girls in the security squad picked up the box to carry it away to lost property there was a commotion the other side of the exit gates. A thin young Hasidic Jewish guy was trying to reach the luggage area and was being prevented by a horde of security men.

"Please, you must let me through!" he was yelling at the security contingent.

"I must get back into the baggage hall." On being told he could not do this, he almost wept with frustration, "but I must, I left the birthday cake my mother made for my wife. I can't go home without it."

Realising that this was the owner of the cardboard box and breathing a sigh of relief that they had not blown it up, Mr. Big, gestured to the young man to come forward. He rushed forward, holding on to his *kipar* with one hand and keeping his specs on his nose with the other, he grabbed the box and tried to close the lid. His agitation was such that his *payot* ringlets danced around his head and his black coat came open at the waist to show his prayer vest. He was making such a mess of closing the box that one of the security personnel went over to help him and presented him with a properly complete box.

"Thanks be to God," he enthused. "Blessed be His name. I have been rescued," he gurgled as he shuffled out to the entry hall of the airport with his box under his arm.

I also thanked God under my breath that it had not been an Arab youth who had left the box behind. That would have triggered a different reaction and he and his box would have been detained in the security area and neither he, nor his wife, would have been able to enjoy the cake.

From the Beginning, it Went Wrong

I was looking forward to my new job, to the challenge of putting my own ideas into practice. I had rented out my house, sent my books on by sea and packed up as many clothes as I thought I needed. And here I was. I had been met at the airport by the Vice Chancellor of the university, no less, and driven to this apartment they had rented for me. Now the fun started, before I could eat, we had to change the calor gas cylinder and buy some staple foods at a local shop, that didn't look like a shop as it had its shutters closed.

Then I was left alone to get used to my new home. I made a cup of instant coffee that tasted foul and put my photo album on the window ledge to make me feel more at home. Instead, I felt home sick. Had I made a big mistake? Was I going to be happy here? I cheered myself up at the thought of seeing the two British people I had met when I came for my interview three months before. We had got on well. They would help me feel I wasn't entirely on my own.

After a night when I tossed and turned, I set off to find my friends. I knew that their landlord spoke English so felt I could communicate reasonably well. I rang the bell and waited as a Palestinian lady came to the door and smiled at me. "Hello, I have come to see Colette and Paul" I said expectantly.

Her smile faded as she replied, "oh I am so sorry, but they are not here."

"That's ok I will leave a message," I said, thinking they were out somewhere in the town.

"I mean they have returned to England," she sympathised.

I gulped and my heart sank as she explained in simple English that Colette's mother was ill, and Paul had left his job at the children's orthopaedic hospital. I felt bereft but managed to thank her.

I decided to take a walk around the town and buy some fruit and vegetables.

Predictably I got lost and walked in circles in the heat of the day. What do they say about, mad dogs and Englishmen? When I eventually found a greengrocers' shop, I didn't recognise much produce on sale there and had to work out the costs of my purchases in Jordanian dinars and then translate back to pounds.

I'm sure I paid over the odds that day as they recognised a very green addition to the university community.

Next day I went up to the university campus to try to phone home. However, this was not to be. I was told, "all international lines have been cut off. You can't phone England from these phones you will have to go into Jerusalem."

Another nail in the coffin of my hopes. Well never mind, I thought, there is always the postal service. I will be able to receive letters from home. But, just my luck, there was a postal strike in the UK, and I didn't get any letters for weeks. In addition, I was car-less for the first time in 20 years and didn't yet trust the local transport, so was stuck in Bethlehem.

By this time, I was convinced I had made the wrong decision to come to this place and would have booked a ticket home there and then if I had been able. I was finally rescued from my six- week solitary confinement by another British colleague who did have a car and lived in Jerusalem. Thankfully, first impressions are not always correct. I must have got used to Bethlehem as I lived there and stayed at the university for eleven years.

It isn't What I Expected

"Dear Jenny, it isn't going to be what I expected." As I wrote these words in a letter to my cousin, I felt again the despair of being out of contact with my family. I had arrived at my destination six weeks ago expecting to see familiar faces, having freedom to travel and access to telephone conversations with my family in England.

When I came for my interview, I had met people I expected to see again and was happy that there would be some friendly faces. I didn't expect there to be a curfew during which I would be confined to my flat for days at a time with only a few hours respite to go buy bread and milk.

I didn't expect that there would be no public transport to the nearby towns. I thought I would be able to visit my friends in safer areas of the country, but I was to be confined in this crazy place where army jeeps raced around the streets at all hours, where car drivers used their horns at every possible opportunity, where military helicopters hovered overhead, and kids roamed the streets throwing stones at everything and everybody they didn't recognise.

'How was I going to cope with this for the next four years?' I thought to myself, 'what have I let myself in for?'

Now to make everything much worse I had no access to international telephone lines, so I was cut off from all the people who cared about me and what I was doing. There was international phone access available but that was in the larger nearby town, and I had no transport to get there.

I had said to my family as I left home, "don't worry. I will be fine. I've been there and I know what it is like and have people there who can help me." The fact that they believed me, indicated their lack of knowledge of what was happening in that part of the world. The fact that I said it, well I suppose it indicated a certain faith in the organisation that had employed me, but I should have known better.

It was a blow to find that the Europeans I had met six months ago were no longer there. Some were recalled by their employers because they had been threatened by local people and another had been summoned by family members as her mother was ill. Most of my human supports had been taken away at once. I felt more than ever like an outsider.

The fact that I was writing a letter to my cousin in England showed how unsettled I was, as I usually hated letter-writing with a passion, inherited from my childhood when my mother insisted that I send thank you letters for birthdays and Christmas presents. I was much happier speaking to people on the phone, but this outlet was closed to me at present. I wasn't even sure that the letter would be posted or sent, as the postal system, such as it was, seemed in chaos. I had not received a letter from the UK in over a month.

Who could have expected this situation? Maybe I should not have come.

Upside Down

So here we are spending the night, and unknown future nights, in this place that is not our home, with no prospect of going home soon. Thinking back to the moment the trucks set off for an unknown destination. Jorj, voicing all their doubts, suppressed until now, muttered, "I hope we are not making a big mistake."

The news came just after the market opened. Every woman who could walk began filling her basket with food. After all, who knew when they would next have such an opportunity?

Jorj zoomed into the village on his ancient Lambretta scooter. It had seen better days, but it could still cover the miles faster than the even more ancient telephone wires could when harried into action after the handle had been cranked at head office in the nearby town. That said more about the limited telephone service than the speed of the scooter.

"They are coming," he yelled as he jumped onto the pedestal surrounding the war memorial to make sure that all those gathered in the marketplace heard him. "Quickly. We need to be ready."

Nobody needed to ask who was coming. They all knew, all except Jacob who everyone said was a bit simple. His mother nudged him to be quiet and dragged him off up the street and in through their front door.

The street gradually quietened as everyone disappeared indoors to get ready. The place looked like a ghost town with no noise to be heard except the wind whistling through the tall pine trees shading the graveyard. As dusk deepened the entire village gathered in the church with such goods as they could collect in the time available, and then the priest barricaded the door.

They came before dawn, knowing that it was the best time to catch people unprepared, before they were awake.

The village expected doors to be kicked in, to be beaten and cursed and they clutched their small children close and hid their sons in the vestry and in the rafters. The men looked at each other and remembered the oaths they had sworn the night before. "If you are taken, I swear to protect your wife and children." They took a tighter grip on the puny weapons they had managed to find or make. No match for the professional equipment of soldiers.

Imagine their surprise when the men who came did not break down the doors but knocked like civilised people and shouted, "Can we come in?" Suspecting a trick, Adam, the village elder cautiously poked his head round the door, not opening it wide and found that their visitors included both men and women, who looked serious but not threatening. His mouth opened but no words came out, he was so shocked.

"Please come with us," said the man who appeared to be the leader of the visitors "There is not much time. The soldiers are not far behind us."

Adam and those who could hear through the half-closed door, looked bewildered "Who are you?" someone asked, "How can we trust you?"

"Look at us. Do we look as if we are coming to harm you?" The door was pushed slowly open so the women and children could see who were outside.

"We have come to rescue you from the soldiers. The rumour is that they are coming to kill you men, rape your women and enslave your children. Please hurry we don't have much time."

"How do you know all this?" yelled Jorj from the back of the crowd.

"We have a spy in army headquarters who warned us that this village is next on the list for destruction."

As the men began to argue with Adam, Miriam stepped forward and took a closer look at those gathered outside "I would rather trust these people than wait for the soldiers to come. I have heard about this group.

They did the same thing at my cousin's village, got all the villagers to safety.

By the time the army trucks arrived the village was empty, but it was burnt down anyway."

After the usual endless discussion, Miriam's words seemed to convince Adam and the other men; they all piled into trucks, normally used for transporting food relief. There was a slight hiatus as everyone had to leave behind some of their belongings and families fought over treasured possessions, they were not willing to leave behind. As the trucks rolled out, they left behind a ghost village.

A Sign of the Times

The prospective students staggered out of the room in confusion. They had just faced an interview with two women, one Palestinian and one of the new foreigners. What stupid questions they had been asked "Why do you think you would make a good physiotherapist?" What did that have to do with anything?

Comparing notes, the boys expressed their disgust and suspicion that these questions should be asked. After all Ali's father was a good friend of Abu Ahmed, who had just been appointed a teacher on this new programme. Surely that was enough. Daud had pinned his hopes on his aunt who ran a rehabilitation centre for disabled children in Jerusalem. There could be no better recommendation than that!

There wasn't time to talk any more, as they now had to present themselves for a practical aptitude test, whatever that was. What was the point of this? Why not choose people from good families? Of course, giving priority to the boys.

The final straw came when they were ushered into a classroom and instructed to sit in a circle of chairs and discuss what they would do if they encountered an unconscious man by the side of the road. What did this have to do with working in a rehabilitation clinic?

Meeting up at the end of the day, tired and angry, they determined to use the influence of important men in the community to point out to these foreign women how things should be done.

Next morning there was a knock at the door of Jane's office and in walked an impressive man who told her that he had been Dean of Arts at this university for the last ten years. When this didn't seem to impress her, he said pompously, "Ali Hasan is the son of my greatest friend, and I promised him a place on this new programme." Controlling her anger and keeping a smile on her face, she explained that competition was so great for this training that they had discussed the best way to select the most appropriate students with the Dean of Education. "Well of course, you choose the people from the best families, that is what we have always done". Smiling to herself, she remembered that Dr Violet had said this is what would happen but had encouraged her to use these more modern ways of selection.

Soon after Dr Walid had stomped out of the office, aware that he had been bested and not pleased with his own performance, Father Dimitri, the Greek Orthodox parish priest pushed his way into the room without even knocking on the door. He didn't need to do that. This was a Christian university, and his parishioners had the most right to be students here. Surely this woman, who unlike most foreigners, was reputed to be a practicing Christian, albeit a Protestant, would understand the need to favour Christian students?

When the results of the selection process were published, neither Ali nor Daud had been chosen. When further enquiries were made, the two sponsors received the answer "They did not appear to understand what physiotherapy was and their participation in the selection activities was minimal."

This made no sense as they were both good boys and needed important jobs to uphold the status of their families. Complaints went as high as the Vice Chancellor who explained that this was the way things were done in the west and if Palestinians wanted to be seen as modern, they had to accept such methods. He sighed, shrugged his shoulders, and said, "I am afraid it is a sign of the times."

The Value of Friendship

Bright he was not, but that he thought did not matter. We met at the Bethlehem Arab Society for Rehabilitation where he was a volunteer working with the disabled adults who often needed two strong men to turn them and move them.

The Bethlehem University physiotherapy degree programme was based at the same centre during the closure of the universities. Some students needed to be admitted despite the ban on higher education because of the nature of the subject studied, so nursing, midwifery and hotel management masqueraded in different places to keep the students and teachers safe from fines and imprisonment. Our masquerade was in this rehabilitation centre.

Mahmoud was a willing assistant when any patient needed to be moved. He enjoyed practicing his English on we Brits and was clearly delighted by his relationship with us. Obviously, he felt that we rated him highly because we spoke with him.

I knew nothing about this young man's background, until I realized that he was planning to apply to join the next cohort of physiotherapy students at Bethlehem University.

Suspecting that this might be problematic, I sought advice from my Palestinian colleagues, who told me that he did not have the appropriate Tawjihi qualifications for university admission.

"Be careful, Lesley, He thinks he is a shoe-in because you are his friend."

I couldn't believe that this was so, but I was still learning how different Arab culture was from European culture.

I tried to stay out of the adults' ward to minimise my contact with Mahmoud as preparations began for the selection process for physiotherapy. BU admin staff were responsible for checking all applicants' university entrance scores and they forwarded to us those who might be suitable for interview.

Of course, Mahmoud's name did not appear on that list.

The day came when he pushed his way into my office, despite the best efforts of my secretary, and demanded to know why he had not received an appointment for selection. This situation was beyond his English ability and mine to explain in simple English. I called on Ahmed to speak to him in Arabic.

Patient I was not, usually, but this demanded all my effort. "Ahmed, be kind to him," I suggested anxiously and tried to maintain a neutral look on my face that was not too negative.

"He thinks that he will get a place, because he is your friend." Ahmed interpreted for me. After this a long discussion ensued in Arabic with lots of dramatic gestures on both sides and what sounded to me like a huge argument.

In the end Mahmoud shook his head and walked angrily out of the room, looking at neither of us. I looked at Ahmed for some clarification.

"I told him it was the fault of the foreigners. This is the way they do things in England. I didn't want him to blame me."

Thanks, I thought, now I will be seen as the bad one when it is the university who vetoed his application.

"In future I would advise you not to be so friendly with the volunteers. You need to keep your distance and show them that you are above them, or they will not respect you."

This was hard to take as it was not my communication style at all. However, Mahmoud made the decision for me, he completely ignored me every time I came anywhere near, and all the other volunteers followed suit. I had been sent to the Palestinian equivalent of Coventry.

None of Them Knew the Colour of the Sky

None of them knew the colour of the sky. Stumbling towards their destination they had to keep their eyes on the way in front of them. As the day wore on the temperature continued to rise and if they had looked up, they would have seen the golden ball of the sun high in the sky surrounded by streaks of piercing light. But they dare not look up as it would have caused them to slow down and stumble.

This was forbidden by their captors and provoked shouting manhandling and guns pointing at them. They quickly learnt that this was not going to help. It was getting hotter and hotter, and the weaker members of the party were now struggling to keep up.

George and his family, along with the rest of the village, had been woken at dawn by loud bangs on the door and had been driven from their homes at gun point by shouting soldiers, telling them that it was not safe to stay. The women barely had time to wake up the children and dress them in warm clothes. The men gathered food and water as best they could while arguing with the commander and asking where they were going. No answers were forthcoming, and they all set off into the unknown.

Mary was already awake and nursing baby Jack when the orders to move were given. She protested to George that she could not walk any distance as she had delivered this newest baby only two days ago. He looked at her in exasperation as she refused to move, and the rest of the children looked on in confusion. In desperation he took the baby from her and strode to the bedroom window. He leaned out and threatened to throw Jack out if she did not get up and leave the house. She looked at him in horror and surprise, this was her husband of ten years and she thought she knew him.

She could not see through her tears George's turmoil and concern for her and their children.

Now they were walking on rocky paths and goat tracks over the rough mountains in the heat of the day. All their water had already been given to the children and they looked on thirstily as the soldiers dipped into their water bottles to drink. By mid-afternoon some of the older people had quietly sat down and refused to move any further, despite the pleadings of their families and the threats of their escort.

Babies and small children lay inert in the arms of their parents and older siblings as the effects of sun and thirst took their toll. If they didn't reach a town soon, they, and many others, would die.

As the sun began to go down, they reached the outskirts of a town and the inhabitants emerged from their homes and stared in bewilderment at the procession before them. When they realised what was happening, they rushed into their houses and returned with bottles, glasses, jugs of cold water. George saw his cousin, Michel, coming towards him and almost fell into his arms in relief. Willing arms took the baby and children from them and led them the cool interior of a house.

Fires began to be lit and food passed around. Children and grandparents were found places to sleep, and they all sat down to discuss what had happened. George voiced the views of all the refugees when he said, "we thank you for your hospitality. We will rest here until it is safe to go back to our homes." At this he, and many of the other men, produced the keys to their homes in the far- off village. Earlier that day they had locked the doors and put the keys into their pockets to keep them safe for when they returned home.

I had a Dream

I had a dream last night that I was back at home in the village of my birth. I was walking with my father in the olive orchard deciding the best time to harvest the olives and discussing how many people would be needed to pick and bag the olives, how many of the younger children would be free from school to shake the trees. The sun was high in the sky and all around was bright and clean.

As we walked, my father placed his hand on my shoulder and said proudly, "one day, when I am gone, this will all be yours as you are my eldest son. Of course, as part of that responsibility you will look after your mother for the rest of her life." I nodded absently thinking that would be a long way off yet as my father was strong and healthy, and I had not yet finished my training at the agricultural college.

We walked back to the house to eat the traditional breakfast my mother had prepared for us and the rest of the family. I could taste the yoghurt, the olive oil and the za'atar and could smell the delicious scent of the bread she had cooked on the traditional oven at the bottom of her vegetable garden. She patted my cheek affectionately as I sat down on the floor cross legged around the large tray on which the food was displayed. I knew I was her favourite child. She had told me so many times, "my first born," she would say with a broad smile when she introduced me to visitors.

I woke up with a start as I heard the call to prayer and looked around me in a daze. Where was this place? This wasn't the bedroom I shared with my younger brothers, it was a dormitory tent in which twenty men snored and sometimes whimpered through the night. The air was chilled, and my one blanket was too thin to keep out the cold. As I turned over, the bell rang for the beginning of the day and started the whole round of boredom with nothing to do and fear of being taken for interrogation.

I remembered that home was now a refugee camp, from which I had been taken in the middle of the night by soldiers carrying automatic guns and shouting my name. Thank goodness my father was not alive to see the situation in which his family lived with no opportunity to visit, let alone, harvest the olive crop. My responsibility to my mother was also over as she had died of a heart attack the first time that soldiers had invaded our home. I had managed to obtain scholarships for two of my brothers to study in Ukraine, one in medicine and the other mechanical engineering but I missed their cheerfulness. Two of my sisters were safely married to men from good families in the town nearby to our home and had already started their own families. The younger children were being looked after by my uncle until I finished my prison sentence.

All through that day I slowly began to feel different somehow. I began to reflect on my situation here. There was no point in being angry all the time, refusing to eat, refusing to participate in prison life, not helping the younger prisoners to continue with their learning. This was only making my life worse. It was turning me into a bitter man. A university teacher had set up a school and college in a nearby tent and was desperate for help from any who had some qualifications. I could use the skills I had learned in college. I could help the kids plant seeds that would mature into vegetables that would vary the monotony of the food our jailors provided. I would continue my own education; learn how to combat occupation using advocacy and peaceful resistance rather than violence.

This Christmas was Going to be Different

For a start I was no longer at home, home being the UK. This Christmas I was spending the holiday period in THE place to be – Bethlehem, where it all started. The university semester ended on the Friday before Christmas Day, but nobody seemed to be getting excited about it. This seemed very odd, maybe it was a feature of being there all year round and walking past the Church of the Nativity in your lunch break.

Visitors from the UK were coming to stay. Well, they were Irish but living in England. A turkey had to be purchased and cooked but When I asked where to get one, I was told, "you go to the poultry market, point at the one you want, and the man will ring its neck. Cut off the head and feet and give it to you, still warm in a plastic bag. You can't get fresher than that."

I wasn't keen on such graphic detail, having been brought up in a city where you went to the supermarket and got a turkey already prepared. Israeli friends came to the rescue, Jack was a butcher, and he was very happy to buy a turkey, kill it, prepare it, and leave it to hang for five days in the prescribed manner. I just had to drive to Tel Aviv to pick it up.

All went fine until we returned to Bethlehem on Christmas Eve afternoon. The Israeli authorities had slapped on a curfew, and we were unable to get to my flat. Having tried in vain to argue my way through the checkpoint we left my car by the side of the road with all the other late entrants to Bethlehem and got out to walk carrying bags of fresh vegetables and a huge turkey. Oh, I forgot to say we also had a small terrier dog on a lead to escort us. My British colleague had been invited by her family in England to join them for Christmas. Of course, she couldn't take the dog, you can guess who she left him with.

Everything turned out well, in the end, and we all sat down to eat, a veritable United Nations of people from Ireland, Scotland, England, France, Netherlands and Belgium plus a stray American we had picked up on a visit to Wadi Qelt.

He didn't know any more details than where my building was and that my name was Lesley. In true American style he bluffed his way into the building and asked about me. "Ah," said my downstairs neighbour, "that is the English woman who works at the university. Top floor, last door on the right."

We managed to get tickets to the midnight service in the Church of the Nativity and came away in the early hours of Christmas morning and yes, the bells do really ring out at that time. My ears can testify to that. I was glad we had arranged our dinner for Christmas Day evening.

Would She Come Again?

I first met Georgina in the late 1980's when she came on a visit to Bethlehem for the charity Action around Bethlehem Children with Disability (ABCD) with Val. They were visiting the Bethlehem Arab Society for Rehabilitation and staying with Edmond Shehadeh, the director of the centre. This visit coincided with the declaration of the State of Palestine by Yasser Arafat.

She and Val needed to get to a meeting in Jerusalem and I offered to drive them. On arriving at the Shehadeh's house Val and Georgie informed me that we had to make a detour up the hill at Bet Jala to the disabled children's orphanage to check they were ok as there was a curfew and Edmond couldn't leave his house.

We duly found the centre and knocked on the door to find that the house mother had no key to the food cupboard, which was in the possession of the White Sister who lived in a convent down the hill in Bethlehem. We set off to get the key, but this was to prove no easy matter. We had to argue our way through an Israeli army roadblock to get to the convent and then no-one would let us in. Fortunately, a De La Salle Brother from the next-door school saw our predicament and remedied the situation by whistling towards the window of the sitting room at the convent. The window opened, an explanation was made in Arabic, and we received the key which was to be taken up to the orphanage. After all this we made our way to Jerusalem. During all this Georgie was amused but not fazed.

At the end of the day, our trip back to the Shehadeh's house was equally exciting as we argued our way through another army roadblock by "explaining" we had to check on the disabled children. We joined a column of cars heading up the hill to the Israeli settlement at the top of the hill and discussed how we might take advantage of our escort to get to our destination.

As the cars swept up the hill we followed at the back and then peeled off to the left at the turning to the Shehadeh's house.

It is to Georgina's credit that her first visit was not her last and she made many more trips. She said that her concern about the disabled children at the BASR was based on those she met on that visit who were of a similar age to her own youngest daughter.

Jaffa Oranges

I look back to the days when my rooms were full of laughter. Those were the days when a huge extended family lived here. A blind old grandfather sat in a corner of the courtyard smoking his narghile, chatting to other old men and waiting for their coffee and arak to be brought out to them. His wife was in the kitchen with the other women, not really cooking these days but supposed to be supervising the young girls making bread. Sons were out in the orange orchards picking the ripe fruit and burning the remains of the branches and leaves, some were returning from the market after selling their oranges and grapefruits to Turkish soldiers on leave. Wives and daughters in law chattering and singing together as they washed vegetables and prepared fish for the family supper. Kids home from school seeking treats to keep their hunger at bay being shooed out to play in the courtyard.

Now my family and I are more subdued, fewer male voices ring out as those old enough for military service have been pressed into the Turkish Army to fight. Turkey has allied herself with Kaiser Wilhelm and his Prussians against the British, Australians, French and, latterly, Americans. Across the Empire, men are being forced to fight against an enemy, not theirs. We want our boys to come home soon. The olive harvest needs their strong arms and backs.

Outwardly this house is still the same, but we are now under new management. The war has ended the Ottoman Empire and the British are here to stay. I know that it will not change much for me but there are rumours of immigrants pouring into the country from Europe and arguments between different groups about who has rights over which pieces of land. Many are praying that they will not reach here, but I am afraid they will. My humans just want to get on with growing and selling their oranges, now that most of the boys are back home.

They tell stories of deserting their regiments and walking home the many miles through the hills and valleys of Palestine.

My rooms are emptier than they were as younger members of the family emigrate to North and South America but there are still enough people living here to keep the business going. I am still surrounded by my orchards and business is brisker as groups of Jewish immigrants are building a town just north of here on an ancient site called Tel Aviv.

War has again come to shake my walls and shatter my windows. as I knew it would. My family never thought the British would fire on us, but they did because we were part of the Great Arab Revolt and the British wanted to keep peace between us and the Jews in Tel Aviv. I know that I felt betrayed as did my family. Fortunately, we were not blown up as was the house next door. So many people are homeless, where will they go?

Our town is not so important now as a port has been built, linked to Tel Aviv. This means that we now deliver our fruit there to be exported and of course it costs more money. Today I felt the crunch of tanks and jeeps as my family were told they are now part of the State of Israel and we buildings are being taken over by the military authorities. Instead of farmers I am inhabited by soldiers, none of whom speak to me in Arabic.

There are fewer people around who are prepared to look after me and I am becoming quite dilapidated. When I look around, this is true of many other houses and factories. We are told that there is no money for renovations and more and more people are leaving. We have become like a ghost town.

There came a day when I was no longer a dwelling place, a family home, but an art gallery and become quite gentrified. Many visitors pass through my doors each day, but it is lonely at night when everyone has gone home. I guess humans like to watch a little destruction. Sandcastles, houses of cards, that's where they begin, but they end with empty lonely buildings with no people.

I Want to do Something Improbable

"What do you mean?" her brother, Baruch, asked as he relaxed at home, enjoying a day off from his military service. He sat by the window wolfing down his mother's cooking and gratefully getting his washing done.

"I'm tired of doing the same old things and seeing the same old people every day, week in and week out."

Hannah is an Israeli living in French Hill and all her friends are Jewish classmates from her school and her synagogue in West Jerusalem.

Then Hannah said something that made her family open their eyes wide as they knew she was a city girl.

"A woman came to my school yesterday and invited us to go on a Youth Encounter trip into the desert at the end of the month."

"That sounds good," her mother, Miriam sighed with relief that this was the extent of the thing that her daughter wanted.

But then Hannah continued, hesitantly, "we will be sharing the weekend with Arab students from the Rosary Sisters School in East Jerusalem," then added not meeting anyone's eyes but managing to explain herself, "I want to meet some Arab teenagers."

"Oh no," whispered her mother in shock.

Now this latest fad of her daughter's was not just unlikely to happen, but almost impossible to accept.

Baruch laughed, "you can forget that. Abba won't allow you to go."

That evening there was a big family discussion about the whole issue. Baruch brought his experience of seeing Arab girls when he was on duty in the Old City, Miriam brought decades of mistrust of Arabs and Hannah's father brought his political feelings about the corruption of the Palestinian Authority. Hannah fought her corner by quoting her schoolteachers on the need to be tolerant and the need to understand other cultures. In the end they accepted the situation and Hannah was allowed to go on the trip, but her father said, "don't make friends with any Arab girls, just meet them and then forget them."

Hannah went with some trepidation and initially kept to her own community. However, the organisers arranged for the girls to trek across the desert on camels, two girls to each camel, riding and leading the camel alternately.

Hannah was paired with an Arab girl called Mary who was equally apprehensive. At first, they did not speak to each other more than necessary but after a while curiosity got the better of them and they began to ask questions about each other's lives. Each was surprised about the similarities in their schools, religious activities, family dynamics and personal aspirations. Prior to the Youth Encounter neither had ever spoken to anyone from the other community.

Eventually they began to talk about the history of their communities. Hannah found out that Mary's family originally came from the Galilee but had to flee from there after the *Nakba* (the Catastrophe) in 1948. Mary discovered that Hannah's grandparents had immigrated to Israel to avoid Hitler's persecution of the Jews in Germany. As Hannah spoke about the Israeli War of Independence in 1948, Mary realized that it was what her people called the Catastrophe. The girls both found this hard to deal with but were given opportunities and help to explore their feelings and despite the issues that separated them, slowly began to like each other.

They both went home to tell their families that they had made a friend from the "other side". This was not well received by either family. Both sets of parents said, "don't expect our families to visit each other and don't you put yourself in danger visiting the other side." Despite this opposition the girls managed to keep in touch on Facebook.

In the turbulent political and cultural melting pot that is Jerusalem, it was unlikely that they would meet again face to face and difficult to believe that they would become friends.

Rent a Family

"How many children do you have?"

I was getting tired of being asked this by the families of my students. It seems to be a flaw in my character that I say "None." The response to this is usually "*Haram*. Poor you." This has never seemed to be a problem in my life before, but it is now.

Nasser, a student from Nablus, came up with a possible solution to my problem when he said, "*ya doctora*, don't say you have no children. We, your students, are all your children."

"Thank you *Habibi*," I replied as I slyly asked him, "so, how many children do I have?"

He thought for a moment, silently counting, "there are twenty of us and another twenty on the upgrade programme, although some of them are a bit old to be your kids."

I looked at him with a twinkle in my eye, "is that number possible, even if I were a Palestinian woman, married at 14 years old and was pregnant every year?"

He thought for a while and then sighed, "no, even for a Palestinian mother that is too many."

I discussed my dilemma with my English neighbour who was married to the son of a prominent local Christian family and knew everybody, "it is no good, you will have to marry a Palestinian."

"Even if I do, I think it is a bit late to have kids."

Her eyes opened wide as if struck by lightning.

"I know what we can do. You could rent some kids from a Palestinian family up in Lebanon. That is far enough away to escape detection. You could show family photos of your kids. Provided they are a bit western looking you could get away with it."

"How will I explain the fact that they are not here with me?"

"You will have to say that you and their father are divorced, and his family retained custody of the children."

"But everyone will still pity me and say, *Haram*, poor you. So how is that better than saying I have no children?"

People who Travel are Always Fugitives

Travel is supposed to broaden the mind but that depends on your state of mind when you leave home. I left home because I was tired of being pitied after he left me. We had been married for twenty years and had three wonderful children together. They were all grown up now, living independently, married with children of their own. None of them needed me and I had no skills to find meaningful work for myself. I felt that I had no future in the UK but didn't know where I could go. Then I saw the advertisement.

In my local church magazine, I saw an advert for a job at the Princess Basma Centre for Disabled Children. I read that the Centre was on the Mount of Olives in Jerusalem. The Director needed an English-speaking secretary as many of their supporters were in English-speaking countries.

I wrote off to the address given and received a speedy reply. After an interview at the Save the Children office in London I was ready to go. I think they were surprised that I didn't ask many questions.

What I didn't really realise, was that this place was on the Palestinian side of Jerusalem. I couldn't possibly have understood the implications of that, but I was to find out what that meant over the next ten years.

Now I had to tell my children where I was going. As expected, they were not thrilled at the idea of me going to work in such a politically unstable place but eventually, they understood and accepted my reasons for wanting to begin a new life.

I rented out my house having been advised by a friend working in Oman not to sell it, stored in the loft what I wanted to keep safe and packed what I thought I might need in a Middle Eastern country. My three suitcases were allowed because of a British Airways excess baggage allocation and a tea chest full of books and household equipment had already gone by sea to arrive at Jaffa.

As the plane took off from Gatwick, I felt that I was fleeing from hell and escaping from the captivity of my wasted life. I no longer needed to live in hiding from myself. I was ready for a new adventure.

The People Upstairs

I needed to find somewhere else to live because the view from my balcony in Bethlehem towards the Bet Sahour valley was being blocked by the new apartments being built next door. When I asked around, the owner of the garage where I serviced my car said he might be able to help.

"There is an empty apartment above where my parents live," he said, "it is available until my elder son marries."

We eventually agreed a price per month after I had been to see the place and I moved in six weeks later. What nobody told me was that Ahmed's father was the local mukhtar, the leader of the Islamic community in that part of town. This meant that he could be consulted day or night to make peace between warring members of families and organisations. As the weather was usually warm, except for three months in the year, these meetings generally took place out of doors in their front yard. It was through this yard that I and my visitors had to pass before I could enter my flat.

The first time I had to walk through a group of Muslim men, I didn't know where to walk, where to look or if I should greet anybody. However, I eventually got used to this and managed to moderate my behaviour and dress when passing through the "lions' den," but this proved too much for some of my visitors. Despite my pleas to appear respectable to my Muslim landlord who lived downstairs, my western visitors continued to arrive wearing short shorts and carrying packs of beer.

But why I was so concerned about this. This wasn't my culture. Why should I worry? After all I paid the rent regularly and didn't play my music too loud and they knew that I was a respectable woman who worked at the local university.

Then a local friend explained to me, "in Arab society you needed to be seen as a morally good person to be considered a good teacher. They will expect you to behave as they would expect a respectable Muslim woman."

Well, I thought this might prove to be a problem when male friends came to stay from the UK. What was I going to do about this?

I decided to consult local Christian friends about how I could meet this challenge. "Well, it is allowed for cousins to visit and to stay. How many cousins do you have?"

"Shall I tell people I have only female cousins? Or shall I pretend that these guys who come to visit are my cousins?"

"If I were you, I would pretend. It will make life simpler."

This is what I did. I swallowed my scruples and the people downstairs believed that I came from a large family with lots of male cousins. As all westerners look alike to Arabs my reputation was safe and my visitors, both male and female, continued to visit from the UK.

The House is Silent Now

This house used to be full of laughter and noise. It had been the home of the Kattan family. Ten children had been born here in this village, six girls and four boys, although only five of them survived to adulthood. Her heart wept when she remembered the fevers, the gunshot wounds and the bombs that had fallen.

Her beloved eldest son Samir had been caught in a bomb blast at the factory where he worked. Her beautiful daughter Mariam, newly married and so much in love, who had succumbed to the measles. She couldn't bear to think back to the other bad things that had happened. It was too upsetting.

She began to smile, despite herself as she remembered all the children's paintings fastened to the fridge door. Seema had been so talented. Her teacher wanted her to go to the college in the nearby town but how could they afford to pay for that for one child and not for all the others. Seema had swallowed her disappointment and worked in the local market but kept her artistic skills honed by her involvement in the Easter festival each year.

Jorg was the practical one, he could take any piece of machinery apart and put it back together in a better state that it had been before. His skills had kept the old family car on the road for decades longer than it should have been roadworthy. He had been the first one to emigrate to the States. His father-in-law had a cousin who owned a garage in Michigan and was looking for a new partner. Gradually they had all left, some to the USA, some to South America and some to Australia.

At first, they returned to their homeland each summer for a holiday and regularly sent home money that the rest of the family used to improve the house. Indoor bathrooms had been built with showers and western toilets. Modern kitchen appliances had made her life so much easier, and the new car made it up the hill without them having to push it halfway up.

The modernized, enlarged house became a prison to Hind and her husband. They rattled around in it like peas in a drum. Then one day when she looked at him, Sami had aged, it seemed in a flash that this had happened. He became more and more disabled until she could not care for him alone and Seema moved back into the village to help her. She said she could work online from anywhere, so the village was just as good as the town. The day Sami died was like a reprieve. She wasn't supposed to think like this, she was a devoted wife.

It wasn't accepted at all that caring for her husband had been anything but joyful. She felt like a different woman.

Seema, recognising the change in her mother, suggested selling the house and emigrating to Michigan. Every letter Jorg wrote home urged his mother to come to live in the home of the brave and the land of the free, as he called it.

Finally, she had agreed, and the furniture was given away to cousins and nephews and nieces. All that was left was the mattress she had slept on last night. She had a last walk round the house while she waited for Seema to collect her. The memories crowded into her mind, both good and bad and she had a momentary regret that she was leaving but no, the house was silent now and she felt like a stranger here.

Too Many Visitors?

It was the best of times. It was the worst of times. We had been together for a month. My father had been visiting from England. It had been a great visit, travelling in Galilee. Now he was flying home. We were on our way to the airport.

We walked expectantly up to the check-in desk in plenty of time for the flight. The look on the face of the check in clerk clouded as she examined the ticket and sighed. "You have missed the flight. It took off an hour ago."

"How come? The time of take -off is on this ticket."

"There was a change of plan. We notified everyone on the flight." Eventually she admitted that they hadn't called my house in Bethlehem and was persuaded to book my father on the next day's flight.

My dad turned to me, "what do we do now?"

I wasn't quite sure but knew that my friend Jackie would know what to do. Sitting in her kitchen, drinking Turkish coffee she made a hotel reservation for Dad at a comfortable hotel on the Tel Aviv seafront.

"You will like it. It is where my mum and dad stay when they come to visit."

Having deposited him there and arranging for Jackie's daughter to take him for dinner that evening I took stock of my next task. I was saying goodbye to dad and within a few hours was welcoming two friends flying in for a trip to the Dead Sea. I had it all worked out but hadn't banked on this holdup.

Within a few hours I was back at Ben Gurion, this time in the Arrivals Hall. Packing their luggage into my car I tried to explain my dilemma. I would drive them to Bethlehem and leave them there. We could eat dinner at the kebab house up the hill from my apartment and I would head off back to Tel Aviv next morning. Not a good start to a holiday, but the best I could do.

All worked according to plan, my father had enjoyed his dinner with Dina, an attractive young lady, and the next morning had walked along the beach in the morning sun. Today we were on time for his flight. I said goodbye and hugged him before driving back to Bethlehem. My guests had spent a happy morning walking to Manger Square and exploring the Church of the Nativity. It had been the worst of times, but eventually turned out to be the best of times.

Where am I?

The pungent smell of Turkish coffee woke him up bringing back memories of his mother heating the coffee pot and stirring in the sugar. It was usually associated in his mind with the rich smell of olive wood burning. He lay there comforted by the smells of home and childhood. His nose twitched as he then smelt the spiciness of *zaater*, olive oil and home- made bread. He thought "Oh good, mother is awake, and breakfast is on its way.

Then he began to experience other sensations, tactile and auditory sensations that were contrary to feelings of home. They were not comfortable at all. When he tried to rise from the bed, he found that he could not as his arms and legs were restrained by something. This evoked a sense of panic and he wondered where he was.

At this point he caught a whiff of raw sewage, mixed with the sweet smell of rotten food, especially the smell of tomatoes in there somewhere. He was certainly not at home. There no unpleasant smells were experienced. Where was he? As he became more awake, he heard the voice of the *muezzin* calling the faithful to prayer, so he must be somewhere near a mosque. In a Muslim area. He also heard the noise of a donkey clip clopping nearby and the sound of bells. Of course, he was in Gaza but why was he restrained?

Then other things came back to him. He had been patrolling near the Gaza border with his platoon when Palestinian soldiers appeared from nowhere and shot at him and his companions. Then someone or something hit him on the back of the head, and everything went blank.

He realised he had been captured on the border by Hamas soldiers when he was searching for tunnels leading from Gaza into Israel. They had obviously found the tunnels, and this is where the Hamas guys had appeared from. What had happened to the rest of his platoon?

Had they escaped or was he the only one captured? What did they think had happened to him?

So, he was a prisoner. He began to panic remembering stories about previous Israeli soldiers who had been kidnapped by their enemies. How long it had taken before they finally returned home and what had they suffered in captivity? What would his family be going through, especially his mother? They would be thinking the worst. How had he been overpowered and how could he escape?

As he smelt the coffee again, he began to feel more optimistic. Perhaps they would give him some coffee. He began to lick his lips in anticipation. His stomach began to rumble. Things couldn't be so bad if they made such good coffee.

The Sweetest Taste

Long practice has taught me that one pleasure leads to another, and this became even clearer on a recent trip to Nablus. The Old Testament name for Nablus is Shechem and it is where Jesus met the Samaritan woman at the well. There is still a small Samaritan community living on the top of Mount Gerazim, one of the two high points that surround the city.

The reason for driving via *Wadi Nar* (the Road of Fire) across the desert, instead of through Jerusalem, the more direct route, was the presence of a colleague from Gaza, who did not have permission to pass through the road-blocks in Jerusalem. We were visiting the city of Nablus to discuss the possibility of clinical placements for our students with local hospital administrators.

Because we came the longer way round, we had needed an early start and were beginning to feel hungry. The journey was not too unpleasant with the smell of lemons and oranges in small orchards, giving rise to mouth-watering sensations that were almost tastes in themselves.

Coming closer to Nablus we feasted our eyes on the bakeries putting out their wares, most important among them the local delicacy of *kunefe*. This is made from honey and cheese. It tastes like nectar and contains more calories per bite than you want to know about. We all drooled at the smell and anticipated taste as we drove past. Normally we might have bought some and eaten it in the car before arriving at the meeting. In fact, we might even have been offered it by our hosts along with cups of sweetened Arabic coffee. Sadly, this would not happen today, as it was the middle of Ramadan, during which time all good Muslims fasted until sunset.

Muslim colleagues always told us that fasting during Ramadan was not binding on non-Muslims and that believers gained more merit by watching us eat while abstaining.

But who could indulge in something so delicious when you knew your colleagues were watching with sidelong glances? It might increase the anticipation for them but made the sweetness turn to ashes in your mouth.

Sitting in the boardroom at St Luke's Hospital, the meeting seemed to go on for ever and my fingers kept reaching out for the absent glass of water I was usually offered with my coffee. This was made even more frustrating because of the wonderful smells from the bakeries all around and I am sure that many of us were fixated on that rather than concentrating on the words being spoken.

Eventually we were released from this bondage, and all whispered, "*Al hamdulillah*. Thank God" under our breath as we got into the car.

Winding our way through the streets of the Old City, my Arab American colleague turned to her fellow Muslim from Gaza and said "Mohammed, I think we might be forgiven if we shared a piece of *kunefe* with our Christian colleagues, don't you?" He didn't need any persuading and leaped out of the car and ran across to the nearest bakery.

Expecting us to save the sweet until the proper time, the baker had wrapped up the goodies in swathes of tissue paper. We did wait, just until we exited the city and were able to park by the side of the road with no houses in sight before we tore off the wrappings and dived in.

As we wiped our hands on the tissue paper, Mohammed sighed "That was worth an extra day of fasting. I am sure that there is not anything more pleasurable this side of paradise."

A Christmas Event

She decided to have a Christmas party. The students told her that since the beginning of the Uprising no parties had been allowed. She wondered if that prohibition included her, but they decided it didn't apply to foreigners.

When she mentioned it to friends and colleagues their eyes lit up with anticipation. "Will Papa Noel be there?" her landlord's five- year-old grandson asked. She nodded and gulped and thought what have I let myself in for?

Finding a Christmas tree proved easier than expected. Abu George always ordered enough huge trees for the university public buildings from the Jerusalem Municipality. He thought it a great idea to ask for a slightly smaller one for my living room. Decorating the tree was even easier. After all, this was the place where such things were made. We had bought them every year in England from charities working in Palestine.

The week before the big day was spent getting together festive food and drink. Because participants were both Christian and Muslim, she spent some time wondering how to organise the punch. Eventually she made one alcoholic and one non-alcoholic punch and hoped that nobody dipped into the wrong one.

As the day progressed, more and more people came in and tucked into the food and drink. The level of conversation rose as the number of party goers increased, that wasn't entirely due to the alcohol consumption. In fact, the loudest were those drinking the non-alcoholic punch. She looked around the room in between making sure that everyone was being offered refreshments and marvelled at such a variety of people. Apart from students and colleagues from the university, sat expatriate friends from Jerusalem and neighbours from down the street.

Her landlord paid her the honour of arriving with his wife and she had to make sure they were served from the correct punch bowl.

He looked magnificent in his dark blue *abaya* and black and white kufiyah and sat in state in the best armchair. They stayed about half an hour which is when Papa Noel made his appearance. When they departed, the level of noise rose again.

Eventually most colleagues left to return to their homes and only the students were left. At this point Iyad said "*Ya doctora*, do you mind if we take up the carpet? "

She was mystified but agreed to their request. At this point the carpet was rolled up and Firas brought out an oud and began to play whereupon everyone got up to dance the *dabkeh* and didn't seem at all ready to go home.

The party was talked about in the university for months afterwards and became an annual event. What wasn't widely known was that Abu Musa had intervened with the Palestinian Authority officials in Bethlehem to allow the party to go ahead despite the general prohibition on enjoyment. After all it had taken place in the home of a foreigner who didn't know any better. The other thing, known only to a few, was that Papa Noel was an American Jewish friend of the hostess, from Jerusalem.

Sister Susan

Sister Susan is American, very pro-British and from a well-connected family. She is a member of a religious order that is committed to educating the poor and disadvantaged, especially in under-resourced countries. She teaches music at university where she trains the student choir for chapel services and organises concerts by international artists for local people in the town.

She is particularly supportive of young women from remote rural areas whose life is limited by paternalistic cultural attitudes and geographical and political barriers. She is well liked by her students who talk to her about their personal problems as well as their studies. She will smile and listen closely and ask questions to try to understand but rarely gives direct advice about personal or family issues.

About a third of her students are Christian and the rest Muslim. Most teachers at the university are from the Christian community and the university administrators answer to the Vatican. Sister Susan sometimes clashes with local Christian teachers and staff at the university because she speaks up for Muslims as well as Christians. Christian staff members feel she should support their community because they are a minority in the country.

She regularly walks around the town talking to local people. She has been there for so long that most people she meets have been students or staff at the university themselves or have relatives who are alumni. Her ex–students introduce her to their spouses, children and grandchildren and they regularly invite her for a cup of coffee or a meal. If you go to a local café or restaurant with her, she is never allowed to pay for anything, nor are you.

Sister Susan is seen as a fair teacher, always willing to listen to students. She often manages to get round university rules for the benefit of students she feels have been treated unfairly.

She is a very innovative teacher and supportive of innovative thinking and practice. If you convince her about something you want to try, she will back you against all comers, but if you are a person who lives by the rules, she does not have much time for you.

In her free time, she works as a volunteer at a local rehabilitation centre with young men and women who have been disabled due to gun-shot injuries. She is willing to learn and take advice and correction from the young therapists who work there and takes the younger patients out to visit their family and friends.

She enjoys a day at the beach, talking with trusted colleagues and friends. Although a member of an order whose members are expected to live in community, she prefers to live in one of the university faculty housing complexes and fend for herself.

Even after reaching retirement age Sister Susan has stayed on at the university assisting with administration and continuing to visit remote and unsettled areas with an American nursing sister. Along with many others, I am proud to call her my friend.

Lateral Thinking

Ahmed had to be the one to demonstrate as he had arrived late at the class. He got very confused. What was all this about a red bag and a blue bag? Why mention a blue bag at all if you weren't going to use it? These westerners had very funny ideas.

This was more like it, tubes were more in his line, but why did he have to choose the medium one? Everybody else shushed him and told him to do what he was told.

Why should he now move on to domes, whatever they were, when he had just sorted out the tubes? He hoped they were coming back to the tubes: he liked the tubes.

Medium again, what was so special about medium? Maybe it had to do with the medium tubes, but no, he had to select the large dome because he was a man.

Hang on, what was supposed to happen after he linked the tube to the dome? Nothing?

He realized that the foreign teacher was saying something about lateral thinking and how it could open your mind to new possibilities. What did that have to do with bags and tubes and domes? Apparently, this was a new western idea from a man called Edward De Bono. Except that he wasn't a westerner, he came from Malta. "Oh, then I know him" said Sister Patricia who came from that island "I know his brothers and his sons and his granddaughters."

Well, that made it all clear, didn't it?

Friends Across the Line

She quickened her steps, eager to pray in such a holy place. Having managed to get to the end of Ramadan it was important to pray here. It had been a struggle, but she had made it to the end. A glow of satisfaction crossed her face as she walked with her family along the street from St Stephen's Gate.

Turning the corner onto the Temple Mount she caught the smell of tear gas and the noise of loud shouting in both Arabic and Hebrew. Oh no, it had started already, not much chance to pray now.

A few steps more showed the pitched battle between the worshippers and dozens of Hasidic Jewish men carrying wooden clubs. Out of the corner of her eye she also saw young women collecting stones for the men to throw and cutting up onions to stave off the effects of the tear gas. Stones were flying everywhere, and many were beginning to fall on the ground amidst so much blood.

What was she doing here? She who believed in peace and reconciliation between Arabs and Jews. No matter who had started this fight it would not end well for anyone. Sheltering against a wall she saw a squad of Israeli soldiers creeping forward, protected by a phalanx of perspex shields. Already their faces were grim and their posture ready for action as they prepared for whatever would face them.

In all this commotion, one young soldier seemed somewhat reluctant to encounter the stone-throwing mob. It couldn't be easy to do their job, but they had no choice, they were all conscripts in the IDF. She felt sorry for him as his comrades chivvied him to the front after a reprimand from his officer. In spite of all the noise and clamour, she thought, 'Ya'allah, that looks like Jacov.'

The last time she had seen him was riding a camel in the desert, not wearing all this protective clothing, but in shorts and tee shirt. They had laughed together at the camel's peculiar behaviour. He had told her that his family lived in Gilo, a Jewish settlement on the outskirts of Jerusalem overlooking the West Bank town of Bet Jala. She had liked him then but hated him now.

As the squad pushed its way forward, the young soldier's eyes widened as he saw a face he recognized. No, it couldn't be. She would never be here among all this violence, but it was her.

Dodging the hail of tear gas, with his scarf over his mouth and nose, her brother Adnan grabbed her arm and dragged her over to where other women were sheltering.

"Go home," he hissed, "this is no place for you."

Maysa left the place of prayer with some relief, but not so some of her friends who wanted to join in the fight to protect their holy place. Their families had to pick them up and almost carry them home.

Later that night when the men returned home battered and bruised but triumphant and their injuries were dealt with, Maysa picked up her mobile phone. Three times she started to dial Jacov's number and three times she didn't complete the call. On the fourth attempt, after telling herself not to be a coward, she dialed his number. His voice on the phone sounded tearful and frightened.

She felt sorry for him as she remembered the pushing and shoving of his comrades in the squad and the stones thrown at them, then her heart hardened when she remembered the state of her brothers as they arrived home, eyes red from the effects of tear gas and bleeding from the baton charges.

"I did not know where we were going until the truck pulled up by Zion Gate and they marched us to the Western Wall. Then I saw *Haram Al Sharif* and we all started to climb the ramp. I didn't expect to see you there and almost lost an eye not looking where I was supposed to be going."

The conversation was stilted as each tried to rethink their actions in the context of their intent to promote peace and reconciliation.

They realised how hard it was going to be and what barriers they faced if they continued to meet in the group. By tomorrow all their fellow peace activists would know about their failures to stand against sectarian violence. Nothing travels faster than the speed of light, unless it is bad news, which obeys its own special laws.

The Retreat

"Going on a silent retreat?" laughed my housemate.

"For a whole weekend," I nodded, wondering what I had let myself in for.

"You can't even keep quiet in meetings where you know that to lift your head above the parapet will involve you in more work."

I was reminded of being at a physiotherapy educators' meeting in London with my boss, Pete. He had entreated me not to volunteer for anything. "If you do, it will involve me. It always does."

We were seated at the rear of the room. In fact, on the back row. Pete had advised me to keep my head down so that nobody could catch my eye and assume I was making an offer. This posture lasted until, almost at the end, a most outrageous statement was made that I couldn't possibly agree with.

"Don't rise to the bait," Pete growled, "they are only trying to provoke you."

Too late, my head rose as did my anger and I spoke courageously on whatever subject it was. Too late, I realized that I had been volunteered to be part of the task force being set up.

Hence, everyone's ridicule about my intention to go on a silent retreat at the Lutheran Brothers of Jesus guest house built on the ruins of a Crusader castle.

That first semester in Bethlehem had been chaotic with everything new, language, colleagues, students and, most of all, the rules at the university. My body was exhausted, my mind crammed with new sensations and my spirit overloaded with concerns about adapting to a different culture. My colleague, Sue, had suggested the retreat. She went to it regularly to regain a sense of peace and the ability to focus on what was important in her life and work.

"We arrive for dinner on Friday evening, during which time we can speak to each other and after that we are all silent until Sunday lunch time." This prospect did not fill me with joy.

"Don't worry; we are not left completely alone. There are a few gatherings at which we can sing and listen to encouraging talks from Brother Elia that give you topics to think and pray about later."

This news raised my expectations a little and I began to look forward to the weekend.

I found that mealtimes were the most difficult. One had to sit with other guests and share food from tureens on the table, without uttering a word. It was suggested that one way to achieve this without losing your cool was to try to anticipate what your fellow diners wanted or needed. This seemed to work with most people, but completely confused one German man who was present. We could see his face getting redder and redder as we all passed dishes to hm that he didn't want. In the end, he could bear it no longer and spluttered, "I want the butter."

Not to have to explain myself in slower than normal English to second language English speakers or remember the equivalent words and phrases in American English was a definite plus. I gloried in the inner silence, while appreciating the sounds from the farm down in the valley, birds singing in the trees and the far away traffic on the highway to Tel Aviv.

Sunday lunchtime came far too soon, and it was strange to have to talk to people again. Voices seemed louder than I remembered, in contrast to the silence before. On our drive back to Bethlehem, where confusion and chaos awaited me, I wistfully looked back on my weekend at Latrun.

"Silence isn't always empty, is it? It is not the absence of noise any more than peace is just the absence of war."

How far is it to Bethlehem?

How far is it to Bethlehem?

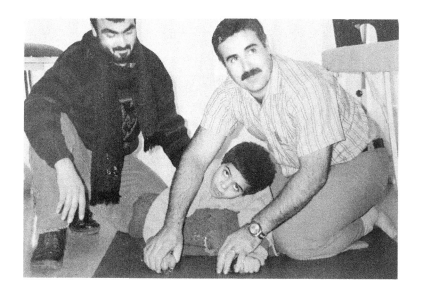

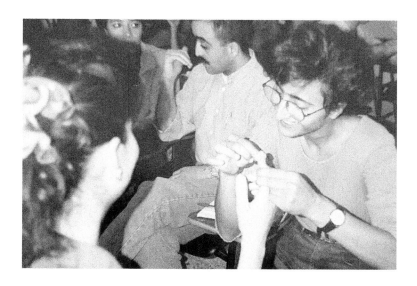

How far is it to Bethlehem?

How far is it to Bethlehem?

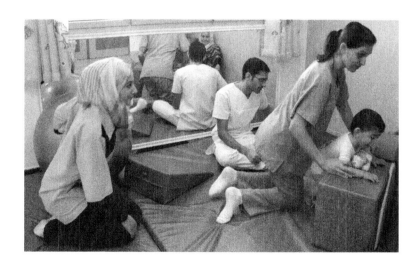

How far is it to Bethlehem?

How far is it to Bethlehem?

How far is it to Bethlehem?

How far is it to Bethlehem?

It was Love at First Sight

We first met at the university Christmas party. I almost didn't go because in the past I had found the evening incredibly boring, same old people, same old talk, same old food. I squared my shoulders took a deep breath and walked into the staff common room and looked round at all my colleagues dressed in their best clothes, wearing dutiful smiles and balancing plates and glasses in one hand. She was in the corner talking to the Vice Chancellor, a handsome man with a shock of white hair and a dazzling smile.

She turned towards me, and I was lost. She was the most amazing girl I had ever seen. Being used to brown-eyed, black haired Middle Eastern beauties, she was a refreshing change with her cap of golden hair and piercing blue eyes. We were eventually introduced by a colleague, and I discovered that her name was Kirsty, and she was an American Quaker here to teach English for a year.

We became inseparable, both in the university and in our spare time and gradually discovered that, despite coming from different cultures, we laughed at the same things, enjoyed the same music and were both irritated by petty rules. By the end of her year at the university we decided to marry, and I would move to the USA. My difficulty was not just getting a visa to the USA but getting to the airport to fly to there.

I was a Palestinian born in Bethlehem and, as such, I was not allowed out of the West Bank without permission from the Israeli Military Government. Early one sunny morning I went to join the long queue at the office on Hebron Road. Though it was moving slowly, those waiting were in good humour swopping jokes and experiences about previous times waiting for some permission or other. An older man from Aida Camp said, "sometimes you can wait for days. It is always worth bringing your lunch with you."

Amid chuckles my neighbour's wife shouted, "maybe you should have brought your wife along to cook for you. If you need to wait all day perhaps you should move your house here."

However, the crowd were not so good humoured as the hours passed and people began to complain and grumble at the officials as the sun got higher in the sky.

Eventually I sat in front of the army clerk and explained what I needed. He shook his head, "I cannot grant you permission to enter Israel until you have a plane ticket to prove that you are travelling abroad."

Now he must have known that all the travel agents were in Jerusalem, the other side of that magic Green Line. However, I reminded him that unless I got permission to travel to Jerusalem, I couldn't buy a plane ticket. Getting restless because there was still a long queue behind me, he shrugged and said, "what can I do? These are my orders."

My heart sank as I thought of my fiancée in New Jersey and the plans she was making for our wedding. This might be one wedding without a groom.

Shalom

We had been to Gaza for the day and were beginning to think about our return journey. The trip down had been relatively uneventful. We had set off at five in the morning so that our passage through the checkpoint would coincide with the exodus of day labourers from Gaza to their jobs in Israel. The sun shone as we drove south towards Hebron and then we took the road towards Beersheba.

There was plenty of traffic on the road as offices and schools started their working day at seven am and finished by noon, before it was too hot to concentrate. After all, most people had been up since before dawn, having eaten a last meal for the day, as it was Ramadan. Most of the women needed to be home in good time to prepare for the evening breakfast, the *"ifta"*, to be eaten as soon as the *imams* in Cairo gave the all-clear for the day's fast to end.

For those of us who had not been up most of the night, the journey was pleasant as we drove by the site of the confrontation between David and Goliath and close by the caves where Judas Maccabeus had hidden from the Romans. The area was so packed with historical and biblical places that I vowed I would spend more time exploring on a day when I was not in a hurry to cross the border into Gaza.

We went through the checkpoint with no delay as no-one was stopped on the way in, only on the way out. After all who really wanted to go to Gaza by choice, in fact in Hebrew, "Go to Gaza," was the equivalent of, "Go to hell". A group of our students were stuck in Gaza without permission to enter Israel and the West Bank, so unable to attend classes in Bethlehem. They were waiting for us at the UN nursing college. More asleep than awake, we reminded ourselves to be especially dynamic teachers that day.

In fact, all of us somehow managed to stay awake.

Although it was touch and go a few times as heads drooped, and eyes were half closed we finished class at noon. This was no mean feat as no-one was allowed even to drink a glass of water. Exhausted students went home to bed for a couple of hours, before having to get up again for the first meal of the day at sunset.

Leaving Gaza was normally not a problem for foreigners who had visas to live and work in the West Bank. However, today we remembered we had promised to take a Gazan colleague back with us and he didn't have permission to leave. How was this problem to be overcome? Sue had lived and worked in both Israel and the West Bank for many years, was experienced at dealing with Israeli soldiers and spoke some Hebrew.

"Sit in the back of the car," she told Mohammed, who was willing to try but expected to be turned back when it was discovered he had no permission.

I was instructed to drive casually through the checkpoint at an appropriate speed, stopping whenever instructed to do so. Sue sat in the front passenger seat, opposite where the Israeli soldiers would peer into the car. I did as I was asked, with my heart beating so loud I felt that every soldier within three miles could hear it.

At the exit to Israel the soldier on duty raised a hand to stop us and I thought, "Here it comes" with visions of Mohammed being arrested for not having permission and myself being separated from my British passport. At this point Sue wound her window down, casually leaned out and said *"Shalom,"* to the soldier. To our surprise he waved us on replying, *"Shalom, Shalom."*

Mohammed chuckled all the way back to Bethlehem, saying *"Shalom"* to himself. I mulled over the day as we joined Mohammed and his family for "breakfast" and thought you need closeness with other people. And how is closeness built? By sharing secrets.

Taxi!

Just a minute! Where are we going? This isn't the way to the airport.

Here I am sitting in the back of a Mercedes taxi supposedly on the way to Tel Aviv airport, but we have just done a u turn and gone back through the checkpoint into Bethlehem instead of taking the road to Jerusalem.

I look at the taxi driver who is a big guy wearing a Muslim cap and a big bushy beard. I didn't notice this when I got into the taxi at the hostel in Bethlehem. He seemed a very nice man with a big smile but I'm sure he didn't have this beard. Am I being kidnapped? I have heard stories about Muslim men kidnapping Christian women, but I am way too old to be considered worth all that effort.

When we left Bethlehem, his English conversation seemed fluent, and we chatted about all kinds of things but now he is tight lipped and grips the steering wheel as though we were going to be rear ended by a tank. Maybe I can jump out of the car before he spirits me off to Hebron and the white slave trade. I try to turn the door handle without alerting his suspicions but realise he has a car with child-proof locks, and I am held captive in this car. What am I going to do?

In my mind I go over all the things I have done, the places I have been and the people I have met over the last two weeks – maybe he saw me going into the Jewish side of Abraham's Tomb in Hebron and that has upset him, maybe one of his daughters has become too independent, because of being a student at Bethlehem University. Is it Balfour Day today and I have forgotten it. Does he blame me for the Six Day War? What has the British government been doing recently? I turn my mind to recent news items. Does he object to Brexit and think I voted for it? Has he mistaken me for an American and is linking me with Donald Trump's recent outbursts?

My heart rate has risen, and I am sure I am going to have another heart attack.

I realise that I haven't voiced any of these thoughts being too busy frightening myself. I turn to my driver and say, "Where are we going?" He smiles and says, "Just five minutes and you will know". This makes me feel even worse until I realise that I recognise where I am. We are turning into the gate of Bethlehem University and pulling up outside the Brothers' House where we are met by a smiling Brother David. He opens my door and helps me out saying "Thank God that we caught you before you had gone too far. I managed to phone Abu Sayid on his mobile and let him know that you had left behind your passport. I didn't want you to arrive at the airport and not need to come all the way back."

I breathed a sigh of relief and thanked them both for their concern. I don't remember much of the rest of the journey to the airport but spent a lot of time reflecting on miscommunications and the deceptiveness of first impressions.

The Weekend we all Became Spanish

He wanted to take his students to the seaside. He had told them what it was like and shown them photos of his childhood seaside holidays. They all sighed and wished they could go there. "Wouldn't it be great?" they said. "What fun we could have."

Some of them had never seen the sea, had never even been out of their village or town. Nether had their parents before them. The problem was not the distance as it was quite close by. The problem was they needed permission to travel that far, and permission wasn't easy to get.

One of the mature students knew someone who had a coach and agreed to ask the man if he was willing to take a group to the seaside. He managed to negotiate a good price and the coach arrived at the college on the Friday afternoon just after classes had finished.

The whole group, twenty students and two teachers got on the coach along with sleeping bags, camp beds and so much food it would have fed an army. Travelling in the bus, singing songs and dancing in the aisle passed the time well as they drove north by the side of the river.

"We must stop singing and dancing when we go through the checkpoint, so they won't want to stop us," said Andy. They all calmed down and sat quietly like tourists, as the language the students had been singing in would have given them away. Heart in his mouth, but outwardly calm to encourage the students, he smiled and spoke with the soldiers, who waved them on without checking IDs.

"Adel why did the soldiers not come on board the bus?" asked Andy. Adel grinned and showed him the sign on the front of the coach. Written on it was 'Spanish Tourist Group'.

They all had a wonderful weekend staying at a camp by the lakeside owned by German Benedictines. They slept in tents and cooked on the barbecues provided.

The sun shone all day and sunsets over the lake were spectacular. changing from brilliant red to gold and lasting long enough to sit and enjoy.

The weather was bright sunshine, the temperature was in the 80's and most of them spent the whole weekend in swimming trunks and shorts and T shirts. Some learnt to swim that weekend, some learnt to sail in a dinghy, and others had time to sunbathe. All had great fun and learnt to relax a little and found out that their teachers were human beings.

So much so that years later they still laugh about "that weekend" and at reunions show each other photos. Spouses and children also see what mum and dad were like when they were students. They will never forget the week end they became Spanish tourists.

Some people say…

Some people say this is God's land.

Some people say God gave the land to the Jewish people for ever.

Some people say it is all the fault of those who perpetrated the Holocaust in Germany.

Some people say the Jews who survived the Holocaust have a right to return to their Promised Land.

Some people blame it all on the British who made contradictory promises to the Arabic and Jewish people.

Some people say it is due to the promises that Lawrence of Arabia made.

Some people say it is because of the Balfour Declaration.

Some people say that they still have the key for their house in Jaffa.

Some people say that they have a right to return to their homes from which they were driven.

Some people say it is the fault of the Romans who destroyed Jerusalem in AD 70.

Some people say that there are no such people as Palestinians.

Some people say they can't understand what all the fuss is about.

Some people can't understand why Jews and Arabs can't share the land.

Some people say they will keep on trying to cross the border to get back home.

Some people say they will treat all people as invaders who approach their border.

Leaving Gaza?

And then there was the day when we couldn't get out of Gaza…
Visitors from Kingston University were visiting the UN School of
Nursing for a validation visit. I had met them at the checkpoint in
the early morning and escorted them to the Baptist College.
Everything pointed to a good day and an easy exit.

The day went as planned with students and teachers behaving
impeccably, exam scripts and course plans approved enthusiastically
and an excellent lunch in a local restaurant. After a discussion with
all the staff I set out to return the visitors to the checkpoint.

At the back of my mind was the rumour heard from one of the
students that there had been an explosion in an Israeli town near the
border. However, the road to the border was clear and everything
was quiet.

Not so when we reached the barrier which had been lowered
and it didn't look as if it would be raised anytime soon. We were
informed, "you cannot pass today. The border has been closed for
security reasons."

I saw the alarm on the faces of the two women from London
as they envisaged the possibility of staying overnight in Gaza. This
had never happened to them before. They came to Gaza for the day
and travelled back safely to Jerusalem where they stayed in a safe
hotel outside the Old City. They tried every trick they could think of
from waving their British passports around to flirting with the young
soldiers, to no avail.

I assured them we would find them a reasonable hotel where
they could stay the night and they reluctantly followed me back to
the car and we drove back to Gaza City.

"And then there was the day we had to stay overnight in Gaza."
Jill and Evelyn were sitting in the senior common room recounting
their Palestinian adventures. The expressions that crossed the faces
of their audience ranged from horror at the prospect of being stuck
in such a place, thankfulness it hadn't been them, sympathy for their
predicament and disdain from those who had travelled to equally
primitive places.

"My heart sank when we realised that we were stuck there,"
recalled Gill.

"And I was sick to my stomach," chimed in Evelyn.

They recounted the calmness of the other expats who lived in Gaza and their reassurance that the border would be reopened the following day. They remembered their surprise at the quality of the beach front hotel and the spread of food presented to them at dinner and next morning at breakfast.

"We were worried the border would be closed for days as we had plane tickets on a British Airways flight from Ben Gurion airport two days hence."

The thought of missing their plane was disturbing as they had heard stories of Israeli security interrogations of people who had come from the occupied Palestinian territories.

"However, next morning when we reached the border the barrier was open, and we were allowed out with no problems."

"I think that was when I understood the insecurity of not knowing if the border would be opened or closed if you were heading to work in Israel or the West Bank or if, like us, you were trying to get home to your family."

The Curfew

The house had a forbidding, symmetrical face with windows that seemed slightly small, especially the third storey row. I had come to this town that was said to be very political and anti-foreign and I was hoping that my fears of antagonism against foreigners were unfounded. I had in my bag the hand-written note in Arabic and English given to me by my colleague, Raeda, to help me get to her mother's house in Nablus.

She was correct in assuming that colleagues at the UN Clinic would point me in the right direction and that people on the street in the Balata refugee camp would be kind to an expatriate female on her own, wandering down the main street and looking confused at the lack of house numbers.

I was already apprehensive about coming to this town where strikes, demonstrations and stone-throwing were commonplace. It had a reputation as the most political and anti-Israeli town in the West Bank and I had carefully avoided it for many months. However, finally I had to visit students on clinical placement at the UN clinic and had climbed on the bus in East Jerusalem with a sinking heart and a fixed smile on my face. This was ridiculous to feel so scared. After all I had been to Hebron and Gaza and survived to tell the tale.

I had been primed by my colleagues at the clinic not to speak to the young men and if I needed to ask a question to choose an older woman to accost. I was followed by all the young boys in the camp with wolf whistles and attempts to speak English.

I had become tired and annoyed with being asked repeatedly "What your name?" "Where you from?" and "How old you are?" when an older woman walking her children home from school took pity on me. Despite my poor Arabic ad her lack of English we managed to communicate with smiles. I remembered my note and showed it to her. She shrugged and passed it to her eldest daughter who spoke to me in English, obviously glad of the opportunity to speak with a native English speaker, "this house is at the bottom of the hill. You must walk a long way and keep straight. When you see a yellow house, you are there."

My thanks were effusive, and I set off down the hill, trying to avoid the sewage channel running down the middle of the street, the plastic bags blowing in the breeze and the stray dogs on each corner. I finally reached the bottom of the hill, having successfully negotiated all material and human obstacles to find a yellow house in front of me. Now I wasn't sure if this was it or was only an indication that I was near my destination.

At this point it became clear to me that there were less people around than when I had set off and I was alone in the street. I had been so focussed on my objective that I had failed to realise what had happened. Hoping that it was the right house I knocked on the steel reinforced door of the yellow house. It looked almost derelict, and all the windows had blinds over them. I looked up at the top floor as I waited for what seemed like an eternity, becoming more and more apprehensive, alone in the middle of this refugee camp.

Suddenly a woman's head popped out of a top floor window and shouted something in Arabic. I tried to reply but no words came out. Then her face light up and she said "Ah, Lesley! *Ahlan wasahlan,* come in come in." With that she yelled something incomprehensible to someone inside the house and there was a sound of feet running downstairs. Within a moment the door was flung open, and I was hustled inside by someone I later discovered to be her daughter who said, "we did not think you would come. There is a curfew on."

Something I've been Meaning to Tell you

It had been a hard week. We had been under curfew for three weeks. All the checkpoints had been closed. Even flashing a British passport and smiling sweetly cut no ice with the young soldiers on the checkpoint. We were all incarcerated in Bethlehem because it was Passover and Easter and the feast at the end of Ramadan all rolled into one. This only happened once every ten years and this year had been it. Security levels were high, tempers were short and gun fingers twitched at the slightest loud noise.

After negotiating the rush hour on the road from Jerusalem to Tel Aviv, I parked my car and walked into Jackie's house to be greeted by smiles and hugs and immediately offered food, the answer to all woes in Middle Eastern culture, whether Israeli or Palestinian. I sat in the kitchen recounting my checkpoint adventures with young soldiers during the preceding week whilst eating meatballs, rice, and salad.

Seeing how hungry I was my friend said, "if you still need more, there is some soft cheese in the fridge "

"She can't eat cheese. She has just had meat," my friend's daughter looked horrified as she walked into the kitchen to give me a hug. She wasn't usually so concerned about Jewish food rules, but the subject had been discussed that week in school.

"Of course, she can. She isn't Jewish," replied her mum in passing, without realising the significance of what she had said.

"What do you mean, she isn't Jewish?" came the shocked question,

"Of course, she is like us, she might not be religious, but she is Jewish."

She turned to me for an explanation.

"This is something I have been meaning to tell you. We thought you might have worked it out by now," said her mother.

We adults looked at each other realising for the first time that this Jewish teenager didn't understand the subtleties of the fact that no Jewish woman would live and work in the West Bank, unless she was a settler and we had made certain assumptions that she would have figured things out for herself by now.

"Why aren't you Jewish?"

This question provoked a conversation about the fact that I had been raised Christian and taken on the beliefs and practices of that faith for myself when I was fifteen. Having been born in Israel Dina had not had to deal with religious differences in the classroom or the playground. She knew that there were Arabs living in Israel who were either Muslim or Christian but hadn't worked out that you could also be European and Christian.

This conversation led to many others over the years about religion and politics in the Middle East. Dina would say to me, "my teacher says this about Palestinians, what do you think about that".

My response, slightly less vociferous, would be, "well perhaps you could ask your teacher to consider this?" This game of verbal table tennis went on until Dina left high school and went into the army.

I did wonder what I would say to her teacher if I met her as a reservist on some checkpoint "Ah, you are that Christian women who has been pouring rubbish into the ears of my pupils" Or perhaps we would have laughed together about our concertina conversation through a fifteen-year- old and gone out for a drink in down-town Tel Aviv.

Party Pooper

"Why celebrate your fiftieth? Don't you want to forget how old you are now?"

Thus said my family in England, but not so my Palestinian colleagues and friends.

"*Maskene*, Lesley, how will you be able to celebrate your birthday when your family is so far away?"

I would have been very happy to disappear to the camping site at the Dead Sea and spend the weekend barbecuing and drinking red wine with a few chosen fellow expats, but this was not to be. Oh no. "We must have a party."

To prevent too much excess hospitality my Irish house mate decided to try to take control.

"Lesley doesn't want lots of presents. Please just bring yourself and we will provide the food and drink." Fat chance of any of that happening.

The momentum began to build and so many people whispered in my ear that they were coming to the party that I expected the whole university and wondered where we would put them all. I began to regret having let out my secret. Two other Palestinian colleagues admitted to birthdays, but not ages, and latched on to my party and it quickly became the event of the semester.

Colette organized salads of so many different tastes I grew dizzy with the smell of the different ingredients. This was nothing like the British version of a limp lettuce leaf, a few slices of cucumber and quartered tomatoes.

I was commissioned to shop at the local market with one of my students. His mother would have been proud of him as he pulled and prodded various vegetables until he was satisfied; we had to buy the best. Being used to buying for two people and taking home the results in a small basket I was appalled to see crates of veg being packed into the boot of my car. This was nothing compared with the washing of said veg under running water. All I could think of was how quickly the water tank on my roof would empty and how much it would cost me to order a tanker in to fill it up again.

The Irish contingent at the university included a very sociable Catholic Monseigneur who was a colleague of Colette's.

He made the mistake of arriving early and offering to help. She set him to lighting the barbecue, knowing that such work was not considered suitable for women to do. Looking out of the back window she prayed aloud "Please God my mother doesn't hear that I set the Monseigneur to do such demeaning work."

I think the whole town came, including my landlord, the local *muktar,* who lived downstairs. We detailed one of the Muslim students to keep him away from the alcohol and he did his job successfully, although said student imbibed a fair amount of red wine after the *muktar* and his party left.

Of course, nobody paid the slightest heed to our request for no presents and the table in the corner began to look like the prize desk for a TV competition. Also, nobody thought that we foreigners could supply enough food, so they all brought their own. We could have fed the whole of East Jerusalem without making much space on the table.

I was kissed three times on each cheek by all the women and by some of the men who should have known better and wished *"Kull sane w inti salme"*. A great time was had by all, and no one wanted to go home. I despaired of being able to sink onto the couch and put my feet up with a glass of wine. It had been a great joy to celebrate with all these wonderful people, but this joy was beginning to cloy and eventually I went to sit outside on the back balcony. I wasn't left alone for long, just long enough to restore my equilibrium and plaster the smile back on my face. Uncharitably I was willing them all to leave as it was not actually fun anymore, it was just 'too much birthday'.

Sisters

Sara and Maryam were sisters, only a year apart in age, from a poor family living in a refugee camp. Both were accepted onto the same training programme to work with disabled children. Sara was very intelligent and self -contained most of the time, but quite acerbic of tongue and critical of others. She was in the top 10% of students and easily grasped theoretical concepts. However, with the children she was reserved and controlling, not able to enjoy her time with them. Maryam struggled with her theoretical studies but was brilliant with the children, very happy, kind-hearted and at ease with them. However, she was prone to emotional outbursts when fellow students, including her sister, teased her about her difficulties with her studies.

Both girls were already engaged to cousins when they began their training. Both of whom had gone abroad to work for three years to raise money for their future marriage and home.

Both sisters were chosen to be part of a group of students offered scholarships to spend a month abroad and learn about dealing with disabled children in another country. Students were asked to choose their partners for this trip as they were to be placed in pairs in different parts of the country visited. Sara didn't want to go with her sister but chose another student who was similarly intelligent and as religiously observant. Maryam didn't mind who she was paired up with and ended working with one of the boys from the group who was from her town. He would never set the world on fire but was eager to learn and experience a different life.

All the students travelled to the airport together, being picked up from their hostels by members of staff. Sara appeared quietly confident that she could cope with whatever happened to her. Maryam was very excited and expectant. She refused to wear her head covering in her new environment as she wanted to be treated as everyone else who lived there. Her sister was horrified and angry that Maryam was not behaving like a good Muslim woman.

At the end of the month, when they returned to their home country, all the students had learnt a lot about working with disabled children that they could use in their future jobs.

Some had resisted being drawn into the culture of their workplace and kept themselves to themselves. Sara and her partner among them. Others had experienced as much of the social culture of the city as well as making good friends among their tutors and colleagues. Maryam and her partner among them. Maryam replaced her head covering on the plane going home and everyone thought her rebellion something she had now got out of her system.

Sara's time abroad had reinforced her feeling that her own culture was superior to anything she had seen abroad, although she had learnt new skills for working with children. Soon after returning home, Maryam broke off her engagement to her cousin and remained single for a few years before she married a man of her own choosing from her town. Sara kept to her commitment and married her cousin on his return home. Both are now living and working in the same town and married with four children each but hardly ever meet or speak to each other.

The Year Without a Summer

We couldn't believe what we heard on the news. The USA and UK had declared war on Saddam Hussein in Iraq. It seemed that Tony Blair read a PhD student's unpublished thesis that seemed to indicate that Iraq had weapons of mass destruction and planned to invade Kuwait. We didn't know what to think, but little did we know how it was going to affect us in Bethlehem.

The university called a meeting of all foreign teachers, and the Vice Chancellor told us that whether we left or stayed, the university would support us. The British Consulate had said the same thing, we could leave or stay. However, if we stayed, we needed to register with the Israeli authorities for gas masks.

We decided to stay and joined the queues at the hardware shops for brown tape to put on the windows to stop flying glass and buying as much food as was left on the supermarket shelves by the time we got there. Most of our friends left and Jack was leaned on by the American Consulate to leave. Being a Canadian gave me a bit more freedom. We discussed things with Brother Anton.

"All of us Brothers are staying," he said, "including the Americans," he chuckled. Being British with family in the military he adopted a savoir- faire approach to the situation. As he spoke, I could see a hint of Ian Fleming about his bearing.

"You could come and stay with us at the Brothers' House, or you could stay in your ground floor flat. Whatever you decide, we will make sure you are ok."

Jack and I made a decision to stay in our flat. After all the two old ladies upstairs had lived here all their lives and they were not budging, so why should we? No one was quite prepared for the first attack. The problem was that the PLO had given their support to Iraq and the Israelis were convinced that they would help Saddam attack Israel. To make things worse the "allies" had refused to give Israel the co-ordinates to bring down the missiles.

We didn't hear directly of course. If we had been in Jerusalem, we would have heard the siren sounding from the Russian Compound which was the signal for people to go to their sealed rooms and put on their gas masks until the all-clear sounded. West Bankers were not issued with gas masks and had to listen for a message from Tantur Centre located just within the Jerusalem district, but on the outskirts of Bethlehem, or from a passing army truck. They had loudspeakers relaying the siren to us. The first time we were out shopping on Hebron Road, along with most of the population when we heard this sound like a strangled cat caught on barbed wire. After about five minutes of people looking at each other and shrugging, one man shouted, "Go home, this is an attack." From whom we didn't know but gradually, and then increasingly, frenetically, people began to push their way back to their cars or rush inside their houses.

It seemed hours and hours that we were confined to our version of a sealed room. Behind where the fridge was located was a space just big enough for two relatively small westerners to sit. That time we came out creaking but cheerful. As the attacks got more often it ceased to be fun and became worrying and eventually annoying. It did cross my mind how the families in the refugee camps coped with all their kids inside one room. I did not envy those mothers trying to keep them out of danger.

I also wondered about the Israeli patrols that still had to move around the West Bank to try to keep order. They had instructions to push everyone inside during an attack and then put on their own gas masks and lie flat on the ground. This became a joke when Palestinian young men climbed onto the roofs of their houses to try to see the Scuds coming overhead, on target for Israel. As they looked down at the ground they wolf whistled at the soldiers and called down insults in crude Hebrew. Fortunately, there were no Israeli settlements in Bethlehem, so we were spared the trauma of settlers driving around the refugee camps shooting their rifles into the air and harassing their Palestinian neighbours in loud Hebrew; warning them what would happen now that the world's media attention was concentrated on Iraq.

We did not take an account of the days and weeks that all this went on. Nobody could go to work, to school or leave their houses except for short periods to get bread. It had to be the women who went out to buy food. Any men could be arrested by patrolling Israeli soldiers. Their tempers were as frayed as everyone else's. By the time things were back to some kind of normality, the summer was over, and children were back in school looking almost as tired as their parents.

Ten Days Under Fire

Today we begin our exile in Jerusalem. We have been advised to leave the West Bank because there is anger at the UK's involvement in the war against Saddam. We wanted to stay in our flat and even began to tape up the windows to prevent glass being damaged during the bomb blasts. Our landlord, who lives downstairs, came to ask us to leave as he is afraid that the young radicals will blame him for our presence, and he has four daughters. He was sure we would understand...

It is three days since we arrived, and in that time, we have registered for a gas mask, an ugly thing that is difficult to put on properly. On the phone to my mother, she reminded me that she had to carry hers around with her during the Second World War. I think the monstrosities we received probably date from that time. To cheer myself up I bought a yellow plastic container to keep it in. We had to report to the British Consulate to tell them we are still here. The British don't believe in evacuating their personnel, they leave that to individual choice. The Americans were the first to go, not surprisingly, they bussed their people south towards Egypt to avoid the bombings around the airport only to find that Saddam was targeting the road to Beersheva. I read in an article in the Jerusalem Post that they all had to exit the bus and crouch down in a gully by the side of the road.

Well, I feel like a hero having survived my first air raid. It goes like this – the siren goes off at the Russian Compound up the road then the hotel's own warning bell sounds and to make sure that nobody has missed all that a porter runs around and bangs on every door. We are all encouraged to hurry to the sealed room, which is in the chapel, where we are counted in and checked for gas masks. The first time it happened a couple from the British Council were found to be missing and still asleep (induced by a heavy dose of alcohol I suspect). As the room could not be sealed without them, panic ensued, and loud conversations took place in Hebrew and Arabic until they entered shamefaced and dishevelled.

I am getting better at this. I keep a sweater and a pair of loose trousers to hand with my gas mask (in its yellow case) so I can dress speedily and run to the sealed room.

Most people seem to have made similar arrangements, but one South American priest always appears in pristine dress with his clerical collar fastened and not a hair out of place. I think he must sleep standing up in all his clothes.

Last night we all decided to photo each other in our gas masks to lighten the mood as we waited for the all-clear. When I sent a copy to my mother, she remembered that her gas mask looked just the same. It makes me more convinced that they have been in storage since then.

Earlier tonight we went for dinner to the American Colony Hotel, one of the few hotels in East Jerusalem that still has some selection in the food offered. We sat in the bar watching CNN, catcalling at the Americans pontificating on the progress of the war from Washington and New York. Even the Americans in our group are as cynical as the rest of us.

I took a chance and visited friends at the Anglican School this evening hoping not to get caught outside during a bombing. I thought I had made it but as I rang the doorbell the sirens started. Great, I thought. They won't let me in. They will have all gone to their sealed room. I was just about to run back to the hotel when a masked face appeared at the open door, and I was beckoned inside quickly.

We are all beginning to get stir crazy and a bit blasé about the bombing so we have decided to go home tomorrow, come what may.

Waiting for Saddam

The colleague with whom I am sharing a room, wakes up with a start.

"Did you hear that?"

"Hear what?" I mumble.

I stir my brain to wake up and listen to the silence, which seems oppressive as we are expecting to be summoned to the sealed room. It seems that another Scud attack from Iraq is imminent, and we are all on tenterhooks. I sit up in bed and look over to the corner where the dog is sleeping and yelping in time to his dream. There has been no siren, no alarm bell and no one has banged on our door, so no Scuds coming over. "Go back to sleep."

An hour later, after tossing and turning and not being able to get back to sleep, I heard a noise. Cars race up and down the hill outside, gunning their engines to beat the traffic lights at the top, as the traffic begins to build up in the fight to get to work. The small tractors are moving fruit and vegetables into the market in the Old City, grinding their gears as they negotiate the steps. Drivers shouting to each other and market stall holders unloading boxes, share the day's news. Children heading for the Freres School chatter to each other as they weave in and out between vehicles and pedestrians, avoiding reprimands and accidents by the skin of their teeth. Mothers watch from windows above and shout advice as they feed babies and hang bolsters out of the windows to air.

"*Al hamdullillah*, Saddam must have been sleeping last night." They are even more tired than I am. They have had the additional worry of listening for gunfire in the narrow streets, reverberating in the alleyways and under the arches, loud bangs on their doors and checking that their teenage boys were safely inside and not out having fun dodging the settlers.

"Settlers on the rampage again, coming up from Jaffa Gate."

"Thank goodness the gate to our compound was locked at sunset."

"Did you hear that?" The unexpected sound of the siren from the Russian Compound causes everyone to scatter and run for home.

"Now, he is mounting daytime attacks" grumbles the woman who has just spent half an hour setting out her wares on her stall.

Back at Notre Dame we are outraged at this change in routine and scramble into track suits. We must be awake as we have beaten the alarm bell. Just as we grab our gas masks and open the door to dash to the chapel, Elias bangs on our door and wakes the dog up. This delays us as we stop to calm him down and feed him before we can leave. The pattering and thumping of feet signal that our fellow guests are not far ahead of us.

"Come on, we will be late and be accused of holding up the sealing of the room."

Now in full flight we skid round corners and down the stairs. The door is still open, and we slide through, out of breath and apologetic, to the loud tuts and sighs of the porter who is waiting to seal the room. Every eye turns towards us, and almost heard comments reach our ears from those who have entered a slit second before us.

"Selfish people… can't get here quickly enough … putting other people in danger."

We smile sheepishly and hide in a corner without saying a word.

Pray for the Priests of Jerusalem

The original quotation from the Psalms in the Old Testament says, "Pray for the peace of Jerusalem" and has been adhered to by Jews and Christians around the world down through the ages. The adaptation of the quote to "Pray for the priests of Jerusalem" was spray painted on a metal door in the Old City of Jerusalem. It caught my eye as I walked through the Christian Quarter from Jaffa Gate to New Gate up Latin Patriarchate Street.

I remember smiling and stopping to take a photo, then thinking "How clever to put it there on a doorway on a street where both Arab Christians and Muslims would see it on their way to Jaffa Road and Notre Dame and also in a place where the discerning tourist or pilgrim might also gain a glimpse of it and maybe the occasional Orthodox Jew from Mear Sharim, lost on his way to pray at the Western Wall."

It caused me to consider who the priests might be. I thought about friends of mine who were Anglican, Catholic, Greek Orthodox and Syrian Catholic priests, working for the welfare of their congregations and helping them negotiate the narrow slippery path of living between Israeli Orthodox Jews in the newly refurbished Jewish Quarter and radical Muslims from the twisting alleys of the Muslim Quarter near the Dome of the Rock.

It led me to remember the time during the first Gulf War, when staying at Notre Dame Hotel opposite New Gate. There was so much fear in the Old City as Palestinians barricaded themselves against marauding Jewish settlers and Orthodox Jews were reminded of similar terrifying times in their *shletls* in Eastern Europe. When the sirens at the Russian Orthodox compound sounded everyone rushed home to put on their gas masks. When the all-clear sounded, doors and windows were thrown open with relief and people phoned each other to check that relatives and friends were OK. We foreign aid workers were ensconced at Notre Dame and phoned all our friends too.

This was when we heard differing stories about the priests of Jerusalem. Some invited frightened parishioners into the churches and convents to shelter. There were also stories of other priests who received knocks on the door from families concerned about the safety of their children. On opening to door, seeing the ashen faces and hearing the urgent voices they brutally closed the door and said "Go home. This is nothing to do with me."

I wondered for whom we should be praying, those doing a good job or those who saw their duty completed in celebrating Mass every Sunday.

The last time I walked past, I did not see the graffiti and turned back thinking I had missed it. Looking closely, I saw it had been painted over although it was still faintly visible to anyone who knew it was there.

On whose orders had it been erased? Maybe church leaders felt it drew too much attention to the Christian community? Perhaps Israeli soldiers patrolling had decided it was provocative? Maybe Muslim community leaders had taken offence at it only mentioning Christians? Who knows? It certainly had had some effect.

Is it Necessary?

It is so difficult to admit one is wrong. Particularly when one has been wrong for a very long time. I had thought that my principles and practices were thoroughly culturally relative but was about to find that this was not so.

It happened this way. Physiotherapy students need to practice techniques on each other before experimenting on patients. Up to this point we had stuck with the cultural norms and kept practical classes single sex. Also, practical assessments in which students had to lay hands on other students to demonstrate their practical expertise had been single sex.

We had spent a lot of time and effort choosing these students, the first to study for a degree in this profession and had determined we wanted equal numbers of males and females. Students came from all four corners of the Palestinian territories, including Gaza. The group was diverse, from strict religious Muslims from Gaza and Nablus to other less religious Muslims who were very modern and dressed in western clothes. The few Christians were swallowed up in the mixture.

I had become increasingly concerned that all students should be able to treat both men and women and had raised the scenario with them of a male patient in pain coming to a clinic and the only professionals on duty being female. We had all agreed (so I thought) that it was not acceptable to leave the man in pain.

My bright idea was that at the assessments coming up we would use one of the more secular boys to model for all the student assessments, both male and female. This would save a lot of time and effort. He was very willing, and I thought we had agreement that this could go ahead.

The morning of the exam, I arrived full of enthusiasm for this new approach, believing we had encouraged our students to move forward in their thinking. It was with a sinking heart I found a notice on the classroom door to the effect that the students were on strike. They had all signed their names, including the Christians. Amazed at this display of defiance from a group with whom I had an excellent relationship. I removed the sign and went back to the office to discuss things with my colleagues.

Our two Palestinian Muslim male staff went to attempt an accommodation without success. It appeared that the previous evening, the Muslim students had checked at the local mosque and were told that what we were asking was acceptable only if necessary for learning or healing. We argued it was necessary but the strictest Muslim student, known by his classmates as "the Sheik," was arguing that we did not determine what was necessary but the students themselves did. Even the Christian students were involved, they were all Orthodox, whose values were more like Islamic ones than western Christians.

We made no progress and decided to refer the matter to the Dean of our Faulty. Brother Joe, although an American Christian, had lived and worked in Palestine for more than twenty years and was wise in ways to achieve compromise.

Hearing from us about the situation, he met with the students and asked them if they would be willing to do this exam if real patients were involved. Apparently, this deal was ok, and we were able to bus in, mostly, male patients from a nearby rehabilitation centre.

After the exam, when we all compared the grades, we had given the students, we found that most of them had failed because they had never performed these tasks on actual patients with such disabilities. What were we going to do? I took a deep breath and decided "This is a good opportunity to teach you about moderation."

"What do you mean?" They all looked puzzled.

I explained that the students had done themselves no favours, by insisting on having patients instead of their colleagues. The boys we brought in were badly disabled due to gunshot wounds and many were semi-paralysed. Because of this the students had under-performed. We knew they could do better, having seen them do so.

It took a while to convince my Palestinian colleagues that raising the marks of all students was not cheating. Fortunately, Brother Joe's doctorate was in education, so he backed me up firmly. When we did this, we found that all the students passed but most of them just scraped through, and the marks were much lower than they normally achieved.

Those who normally scored highly were angry about their grades as it affected their semester grade point average, and I was not their favourite Head of Department.

It took months for students and teachers to learn to trust each other again and behaviour in class was very stiff, having lost the easy relationship we had had before.

We all learnt something about ourselves that day. For me, it was a salutary lesson that cultural and religious values and attitudes will always trump new ideas in education, unless introduced slowly and sensitively.

When I had calmed down enough to think straight, I remembered a conversation with a Pakistani colleague in the UK, before I had set off to Bethlehem. She had said then "Of course, you will need single sex classes and they will not be allowed to lay hands on their male classmates. Muslim women, especially, are not allowed any form of intimacy with men of their own age who are not close family members."

Perhaps because I had been plied with a couple of large glasses of red wine, I was not just optimistic, but quite arrogant that I would be able to change mind sets. She just smiled quietly and allowed me my moment of triumph.

Looking back, I realized that my behaviour was at least racist, at worst imperialist. Everything I had always deplored.

I Remember, I Remember

Sitting still is not something I do very often, not something at which I excel. Despite learning how to meditate with the Trappist Brothers at Latroun Abbey, I am naturally a very restless person. Always on the go. There have been times when I had no choice but to sit and watch and wait, despite wanting to get up and join in whatever activity was going on.

I remember during the First Gulf War sitting in the chapel at Notre Dame Centre in Jerusalem waiting for the all-clear from the Israeli authorities that indicated no more scuds were being launched from Iraq. The chapel was the prescribed sealed room to which we had to run when the sirens went off. We watched each other as we learnt to quickly throw on some clothes before the door was sealed. The prize for the best-dressed person went to a South American priest who looked as if he had never gone to bed compared with the rest of us, rumpled, half clothed and half asleep still.

I also remember sitting by the side of the bed of a man who was recovering from a stroke while two of my students tried to ignore me and find out what the patient could still do. I tried to be a fly on the wall so as not to intrude in their deliberations. I kept my hands in my lap to give the impression of being confident they knew what they were doing.

Because I was a foreigner and they always know better than local people, the watching relatives kept asking the students for my opinion and I kept batting the questions back to the students to answer in Arabic. It would have been simpler just to take over and let them watch, but the amount of learning would not have been the same and the loss of face experienced by needing to be shown by a foreigner would have been hard to retrieve.

I remember the early evening sun gradually sinking as the graduates processed up to the stage to receive their certificates. Each time, a fresh set of relatives dressed in traditional costume loudly ululated their pride in their son or daughter. Those who had already had their moment of fame on the platform with the Vice Chancellor, began to dance in their excitement that they had finally reached the end of their study programme.

It had been quite protracted because of the closure of universities by the curfews imposed during the bombing but the day had finally come, and they were going to enjoy it to the full. No western dignity here, this was a Middle Eastern celebration.

I too wanted to get up and dance, but protocol insisted I sit in my place amongst my Palestinian colleagues and pretend to be professional and calm. The bench upon which I sat was hard and the ceremony had been long but, hard as it was, I had to sit still, albeit with a big smile on my face, as I remembered all the barriers these kids had overcome to get to this day.

There are Never Really Endings

To be chosen as the valedictorian of their graduating year was a great honour and fought over by students in their final year of studies. To be eligible one had to have the best grades, not only in their cohort, but in the whole university.

Between the two girls, the issue was the grade to be given by Dr Hanna, the teacher of the Ethics Course. Basma was a traditional religious Muslim girl from a refugee family in Gaza. This could be seen by her long coat dress and head covering and her skepticism that western ways might have something to teach Palestinians. She had been surprised when her father had allowed her to travel to Bethlehem to study and lived in fear of him changing his mind and calling her home.

Suha was a West Banker from Ramallah, a very modern, westernized city where the Palestinian Authority headquarters was based. It was the intellectual centre of Palestine and Suha had imbibed the modern ideas common among the young people there. Her father had died when she was in kindergarten and she and her mother lived with the family of her elder brother. Despite her brother's attempts to control her, Suha was a committed feminist and regularly involved in political demonstrations and discussions.

Dr Hanna was an Orthodox Christian with very traditional views on health and women's place in society. Suha had already argued with him on the topic of arranged marriages and was told she asked too many questions and perhaps should be willing to listen to someone who was older and knew more about the world. She was concerned that, because of this, he would mark her down on classroom participation, and whilst keen to obtain the best grade, was not willing to sacrifice her principles.

Basma would never argue with a teacher, even one who was a Christian, but started to participate in class discussion when she realized she had said nothing for most of the semester.

One of her friends had pointed out that she couldn't be given marks for participation if she never opened her mouth.

Speaking in public in front of men was a scary prospect but she found her way in when she began to argue against Suha's western opinions, that were obviously not approved of by Dr Hanna, who nodded in agreement and smiled briefly at Basma.

The rest of the class sat back and watched as the two girls fought it out every Tuesday at 11am. The controversy certainly made the class more fun than listening to Dr Hanna talking on and on, as he walked up and down in front of the class without making eye contact with any of them.

Rumours among the student body tipped first one, and then the other, of the two girls all semester. However, when the announcement was made, a student from nursing was given the job. She obviously had participated in the Ethics Course but hadn't been too controversial. This had awarded her an Overall Grade Point Average of 4.8 and pipped Basma and Suha at the post, as both had scored 4.7.

Listening to the winning speech at the Graduation Ceremony they both realized that they were not listening to the words of the girl herself, but her speech had been written for her by the Dean of Students and were grateful that they had not been successful. After all, their education was ending and although they both had to return home, they both had good jobs lined up.

Graduation

We had finally got there. Graduation was in sight. Final exams had been taken and late dissertations had been handed in. Heads down. Marking, or grading as the Americans have it, was underway. Parties erupted all over campus. Good weather was assured. Students tried on gowns and mortar boards, admiring themselves in every mirror they passed.

This was our first graduation. Twenty graduates of the bachelor's programme and another twenty who had survived the upgrading programme. No mean feat for either group as study had been interrupted by what history now calls, the First Gulf War. We nearly didn't make it. It had been so close.

The upgraders were all senior members of the profession. Already holding a diploma. It had been a hard slog for them. They had struggled with the need to do further study. After all, they were heads of departments and directors of clinics. All colleagues at that level were offered places. Some stood on their dignity and refused. Others swallowed their pride and learnt new theories and skills.

One day a week they became students, walking through campus and brushing shoulders with kids who were the same age as their sons and daughters. They suffered the indignity of having their ideas, practices and writings shredded by crazy foreigners, but at the end achieved a degree. And survived, even if it was a close thing, for some of them.

I had decided that I was not going to wear the university academic uniform this time. After all these were the first degree-level physiotherapists in Palestine. Surely that warranted something special. Home in the UK for Christmas, I had been informed that the most prestigious shop at which to buy academic dress was Eade and Ravenscroft on High Holborn. I duly walked in and asked about a gown for a master's degree from Bradford University.

The assistant who came to my aid was not too impressed with such a redbrick, higher education establishment, the shop being just up the road from King's College and was even less impressed when, after being shown the appropriate gown I asked, "do you have a light-weight version, please?"

He pulled his stomach in tighter and sniffed snootily, "madam, all our gowns are light weight enough for an English summer."

"I am sure you are correct but are they light weight enough for a Palestinian summer?" and explained to him the kind of temperatures to be endured there, even at six o'clock in the evening.

The final straw came when I asked for a mortar board. I thought he was going to have a heart attack. "Madam, only the platform party wears head gear at graduation ceremonies."

I hammered the final nail in my coffin when I replied, "this is an American university, and all graduates and faculty members wear either mortar boards or other head gear on official occasions."

He shivered theatrically as he charged me an astronomically high fee, seeming to regret that he had been a party to such a sub-standard transaction. Breathing a sigh of relief, he opened the door. I left swiftly and gladly.

I smiled to myself as I exited the shop with my light-weight gown, hood and mortar board and set off to show myself off in my finery to the rest of the family. This smile became smaller as I realized I would not have room or weight available to take these glorious garments in my luggage. The smile almost completely disappeared when in Jerusalem I had to pay clothing tax on the items, despite arguing with Israeli customs that they were academic dress and not clothes.

My new gown and hood were much admired but were not among the most colourful outfits on show. The prize went to a nursing colleague who had done her PhD at a university in Texas whose gown and mortar board were scarlet with a gold-coloured hood.

All this paled into insignificance as our students began to strut onto the stage of the auditorium and exult in their success. The upgraders began to dance as they waited their turn to shake the hand of the Vice-Chancellor and receive their degree certificate. Was there ever a June as glorious as that one?

You See but you do Not Observe

The foreign volunteer teachers met regularly to support each other in acclimatising to Middle Eastern culture. They would laugh and weep over their experiences in the privacy of the group. Jo began to explain the latest problem she was dealing with.

"I can't see what all the fuss is about myself, but it has caused divisions in my class and the students have separated along religious lines. This has never happened before."

"So, tell us all about it," they chorused as they filled up their coffee cups.

"I thought it was rather nice that a romance had begun between a young man from the north of the West Bank and a local girl from Bethlehem. They look so sweet sitting together on the steps outside the library."

She paused to gather her thoughts, picturing the handsome fellow with his flashing eyes and wide grin and the pretty little girl with her long black hair and shy smile that tugged at her heart strings.

"So, do you think this will lead to an engagement? I guess the families will have to get involved soon."

She shook her head sadly "I am afraid that I think it is all over. The families do not approve. The problem is that he is a Muslim, and she is a Christian. That seems to be not allowed here."

Sue, frowned at her colleague's lack of understanding and thought about joining the conversation. However, she had been working at the university for a long time and was beginning to understand the culture. Because of this she stayed silent a while longer. Everyone now joined in with comments about how it would bring about reconciliation between communities, the need for more liberal attitudes to so-called mixed marriages and stories about friends at home who had married outside their community.

"I really can't see what the problem is, but I know the girl's brothers have actually attacked the boy and the father has threatened to take his daughter away from the university."

Sue felt that now was the time to intervene to explain some basic truths to these volunteers evaluating Middle Eastern society from within their own western attitudes.

"You see everything through your own cultural prism, but you haven't been here long enough to observe the local culture, so don't really understand why this is a problem."

They all started to argue but were interrupted by a student flinging the staff room door open. "Miss, Miss. Please come quickly there is a fight in the dormitory between Marwan and Jorj, I think they are trying to kill each other."

The Deadline

It was getting close to the time Mohammed was supposed to fly to the UK. He had applied to Southampton University to do a Masters' degree in Rehabilitation. All was arranged and we thought we had covered everything. Then came the phone call from the British Council. Mohammed had failed his IELTS exam. What a blow, without this the university would not take him. How had this happened when all his teachers had said the exam result was a forgone conclusion? He would pass with flying colours. How could he have failed?

At this point we remembered Nasser, the middle brother, who had been studying in Belgrade. He had suddenly come home without graduating with a diagnosis of leukemia. The whole family had rallied round to nurse him, but his death came as no surprise. What was amazing was his endurance and patience over the last weeks as he became weaker and weaker. Of course, this had affected his eldest brother's concentration and led to him failing this crucial exam.

We marshalled all the influence we could, called in Arabic "*wasta*," to persuade the course leader to accept him without the English language qualification. Peter at the British Council wrote numerous letters explaining that M's English ability had proven exceptional throughout his course of study and that his final marks had been influenced by family problems. We called in our programme evaluators in the UK to lean on this determined lady. All to no avail. She had heard it all before from students from India and Zimbabwe and Argentina. She was wise to all the dodges that international students used to offset their failures.

With my head in my hands, I said "I am sorry Mohammed. I have tried everything and pulled every string I could find but nothing has worked."

He quietly raised his head, "will you let me try to speak to Dr Jones on the telephone? She might listen to reason if I spoke to her myself."

I did not hold out any hope that this would work but how could I refuse his request. I had seen him persuade Israeli border guards to let us pass on more than one occasion and had been reminded of the parable of the widow and the unjust judge in the Gospels. That woman had not given up and kept on irritating the judge who became so frustrated that he gave her what she wanted just to get rid of her.

I went into the next office because I couldn't bear to hear Mohammed being refused one last time, whilst desperately praying for a miracle. After about ten minutes I realized he had not returned, having failed to convince Louise Jones. Gathering my courage, I crept up to the doorway of the staffroom and listened to the quiet, well -modulated, coherent voice of my wonderful colleague speaking English. As I continued to listen. I breathed a sigh of relief as I realized that he was making progress. When the conversation ended after another ten minutes, he turned to me with a big grin on his face "She has agreed that I can start the course as long as I pass the English language exam by the end of the first semester."

Now we had the green light, he went home to say goodbye to his wife and children, and I drove him to the airport before his permission to travel ran out. We both dealt calmly with the security staff at Ben Gurion. After all, their questions were nothing compared to the miracle we had already experienced.

You Think it will Never Happen

It was a beautiful spring day with a temperature of 28 degrees Centigrade. The hills were covered with wildflowers as we drove by. We had the windows open and Arabic music pulsating from the car radio. As we drove through Ramallah the scenery changed to an urban hotchpotch of old and new and half built offices and apartments. We pulled up at the checkpoint with great confidence as we expected to be waved through after I presented my British passport.

I was travelling in my yellow-plated car with two Palestinian students. They had been on clinical placement in Nablus and Jenin, and I had been observing their interactions with patients. We were on our way south, back to the university in Bethlehem and were about to travel through Jerusalem to get there.

Karim said, "Maybe today they won't allow us through the checkpoint as we don't have permission to enter Jerusalem."

"Don't worry everything will be fine." I said, not quite believing my own words as my heart skipped a few beats.

My confidence wasn't really dented as we had got through for the last five weeks without detection and after all I had my British passport.

We edged closer to the soldiers as cars in front were waved forward. Then it was our turn, and the young soldier took the passport I offered but did not respond to my cheerful smile and greeting of "Shalom".

He handed me back my passport and gestured to the two students to produce their ID cards. They looked at me in horror and prepared to get out of the car and be interrogated.

Our soldier friend was obviously not happy with what he read there and called over his superior who spoke perfect English with a Manchester accent.

"You can go through but they have no permission so they must go back" he said and handed me back my passport. "Go, go, you are holding up the queue."

I switched off the ignition and sat there with my arms folded.

"I will not move until you give these two their ID cards back."

"They must go to a military station to get them back."

"You know they can be imprisoned if caught without their ID card and it can take months to get them back. They are physiotherapy students at Bethlehem University."

By this time horns were tooting, and tempers were getting short, but my blood was up and I refused to back off, we were at a standoff.

Behind me Ruba whispered" Don't worry, Doctor Lesley we can go back. There is a Bedouin road we can take."

At this I said to Officer Reznik "OK, we know we can't go through. Give the students back their ID cards and I will turn around."

Eventually he did this, and we turned around and began a slow trip across the desert where I could not see a road. Ruba and Karim walked in front showing the way and moving aside the bigger rocks. We reached the university later than expected and my car was never quite the same again, but my reputation as a crazy woman was now well established.

Friends or Enemies?

The news was full of Iraq and Saddam Hussein. We were told that war was imminent. The university called a meeting of all expatriate staff and told us that the decision to stay or to go was ours. Nobody would be blamed for leaving. The Americans were pulled out immediately, but the British consulate dithered about what they should advise. In the end we ignored them completely.

In our department we all decided to stay and had begun to cellotape our windows against flying debris when bombs landed. Our Palestinian colleagues were concerned and occupied with plans for keeping their own families safe.

Despite this, Mohammed took the three of us on one side. His usual cheerful face was very solemn.

"If I could, I would take you all home with me to Gaza and we would keep you safe. However, I think it is best if you fly home to Europe. I have a feeling that things are going to get very difficult for foreigners."

The Israeli occupying army gave warning of extended curfews and all those belonging to religious orders closeted themselves in their convents and relied on Palestinian members to buy bread in the short let up times in the curfews.

We wanted to stay in Bethlehem with our friends and neighbours and felt sure that they would not want us to run away.

This was not to be, as overnight our neighbours began to look at us differently. We had become the enemy because our countries were fighting against Saddam. President Arafat had pitched the support of the Palestinian Authority in on the side of Iraq, so all our local friends were committed to supporting them.

It was almost as if the years during which we had lived and worked alongside them counted for nothing. We had become aliens, considered not to be trustworthy.

The suspicions that the local community had pushed to the back of their minds and almost forgotten, that secretly we supported Israel against them, now rose to the surface. Our countries in Europe were fighting against Saddam, having aligned themselves with Israel and Saudi Arabia. We were clearly the enemy.

The atmosphere changed and where once we had wandered freely through the narrow streets of the town and welcomed everywhere, now there were sideways glances, whispered conversations and even a few stones thrown. Two colleagues walking along a raised path overlooking a steep incline to the road below were hassled and pushed by local boys who would previously have looked after us like members of their own family. This seemed a foretaste of what was to come. What should we do?

One of our number did fly home to the UK as her passport was running out and another colleague, visiting her family in the UK, was unable to return. Prices for flights to Europe doubled, then tripled. Scenes at Ben Gurion airport and at the border crossings to Jordan and Egypt were chaotic with huge crowds pushing and shoving their families to the front of the queue.

Knowing we could never face our students if we left their community to struggle alone, a group employed by Save the Children Fund elected to stay, whatever. Half of us came under the British office and the others answered to the American office. It became quite a game, when we Brits were told "You must leave, we said, "We are not going without the Americans" and vice versa happened when urgent messages came in from Washington.

All of us made our different preparations, being prepared to move into hotels in Jerusalem, making a sealed room out of an alcove behind a refrigerator and stocking up on Cremisan wine and calor gas.

In the end, most of us moved, en masse, to the Notre Dame Hotel, just across the road from the Old City in

Jerusalem, within striking distance of the Dome of the Rock. After all, Saddam was not going to bomb the third holiest site in Islam, was he?

Afternoon Tea with a Difference

Meeting for afternoon tea in the coffee shop at Notre Dame was a treat after being limited to Arabic coffee with sugar or Coca Cola or Sprite when visiting friends in Bethlehem. It was an oasis of western culture in the middle of East Jerusalem. Much as I loved Middle Eastern culture there were times when I needed to reacquaint myself with familiar things.

Notre Dame wasn't just a coffee shop it was a hotel, too expensive for me to stay at, a gourmet restaurant where I had been taken for dinner by someone richer than me, a teaching centre where I had worked, a library and a Gothic Catholic chapel.

In 1967 it had been on the cusp between the Israeli and Jordanian armies and its walls showed pock marked evidence of the fighting. The present occasion was made even better by the person I was meeting. Sister Bridget was a nun who enjoyed practising her English and had become a good friend. Service at the coffee shop was always slow, and we both tried to forget that the staff had been educated at Bethlehem University, who was our employer.

Our time passed very comfortably and before we knew it, Bridget said "Oh my goodness, I wanted to go to Mass in the chapel here. Why don't you come with me?"

At this point a small American priest came in looking for her, to ask her to read one of the lessons during the service. With a very wicked look in her eye, she said to him "I am so sorry, I have a sore throat. Perhaps Lesley can do the reading today, Father Thomas."

"What a good idea. I am sure you have done this before in your own parish at home." Before I could do more than open my mouth feebly, he swept off to the chapel.

I looked at my friend "Why didn't you tell hm I wasn't Catholic?" I knew that most of my Catholic colleagues at the university were very happy for me to take communion in the post-Vatican Two environment of the 1980s. But I also knew that many local priests did not agree with this. I envisaged standing up to read and hearing a load voice condemning me as being of the wrong denomination.

Bridget was giggling like a schoolgirl.

"Well, we just won't tell him, will we?" She coached me in the appropriate time and content of what I was to read but I was still worried that I would be found out as an imposter and not at all in the right frame of mind and heart to worship.

We sat near the front of the church, and she poked me when it was the time to read. Somehow, I managed to get through it without making a fool of myself and slumped back in my seat with a pounding heart waiting for a clap of thunder and the voice of God.

All the way through my reading my friend had been clutching herself and trying not to giggle too much. She squeezed my arm, "well done. Read like a good Catholic."

I don't remember much of the rest of the service and certainly could not appreciate the spiritual value of the bread and the wine. At the end Father Thomas came to thank me and I waited for my friend to explain to him what had happened. No accusation, no Archangel Michael with flaming sword appeared and gradually my heart rate went back to normal. After a stiff whiskey in the bar at Notre Dame I remembered that one of my Palestinian friends had told me one could seldom do a good turn for this lady without thoughts of strangulation.

An Inherited Trait

Why am I so ready to offer an opinion on anything (even if I don't know what it means), always ready to open my mouth and put my foot in it? Well, I blame it on my father. It is all his fault.

When I was doing my teacher training, we had to take an Eysenck Personality test to find out if our personalities were extrovert or introvert, stable or anxious. When the results came out, I was off the extrovert scale but thank God I also came out relatively stable. I was so surprised when all my classmates laughed out loud when I refused to accept the verdict. They all said that they knew what I was like on day one of the course.

I was so angry with this verdict that I went home and put it to the rest of the
family, expecting support in my denial of this trait. When they had all finished rolling about laughing and saw that I was unconvinced, they began to give me examples of my extrovert behavior.

"Who always talks to people they have never met before and will probably never meet again, even on the underground? You do."

"Who isn't afraid to complain if food is not up to standard or service is not quick enough in a restaurant? You do."

"Who thinks they can change the world in a day and expects everyone else to fall into line? You do"

This continued to plague me every time we had family gatherings. In fact, it was so unbearable that I decided to leave the country (although that decision also had a lot more to do with Maggie Thatcher and her policies). Because I was now living in a different culture, I thought that my behaviour had changed. Also, I felt that I was becoming more mature and so better able to control myself.

The first cohort of physiotherapy students at Bethlehem University were special to us. They were the first Palestinians to do a professional degree in their own country. For that reason, we knew that many of them would short-cut the career ladder and go into senior positions after graduation. Before that we wanted to give them the chance to participate in professional activities outside their own country.

During their final year of study, we managed to get most of them clinical elective placements in the UK having persuaded various British colleagues that this would be good for their hospital trust's image. We knew it was not going to be easy getting 18 Palestinian students through security at Ben Gurion airport, but the Vice Chancellor wrote us a letter on headed notepaper that he hoped would persuade the security staff not to be too hard on us.

We collected the students in a mini-bus and arrived at the airport. I had given the students, especially the boys, instructions to yell out if any individual was taken away from the group. Maybe you cannot imagine the effect of this number of Palestinian young people arriving in an Israeli airport, but it caused utter consternation.

I think every member of the security staff made a beeline for us. I strutted to the front of the group and having taken a deep breath and calmed my knocking knees I said "Please take us to the Head of Security. We have a letter from the Vice Chancellor of Bethlehem University."

Jewish friends tell me there is a Yiddish word for what I did. They call it *"chutzpa"*. Roughly translated it means cheek. Whatever you call it, it seemed to work and two by two the students were taken off to be searched and eventually they all got on the plane, accompanied by two members of my staff. After the plane took off, I went into the bar and ordered a stiff whisky to let my adrenaline levels return to normal. I smiled as I thought my dad would be proud of me.

House to Let

"I am sorry about this *Doctora,* but my eldest son is getting married and this flat is needed for him and his wife." We had not had a perfect landlord-tenant relationship over the past five years, but this announcement came completely out of the blue. I couldn't think that Ahmed was old enough to get married, but he obviously was.

"How long have I got before I have to move out?" I asked.

"No problems, Lesley. I have arranged with Abu George that you can move into the downstairs flat where Miss Sue used to live."

This news did not fill me with joy as I remembered Sue's difficulties in separating out her electricity bill from the one for the whole house and how often she felt she was supporting the whole family.

Not committing myself to Abu Ahmed, I decided to ask around about houses and flats to let. Knowing what a mine field this was for foreign women I enlisted the help of my friend Majdi. Not only was he the owner of a local souvenir shop and thus knew everybody in town, but his sister-in-law was Scottish and had made him promise to look after me when they had returned to Edinburgh.

I think we must have looked at every flat to rent in Bethlehem. I was very grateful to have Majdi as my interpreter as most of the conversations were carried on in Arabic and at that time my command of the language was rudimentary. I would sit there listening to brisk conversations until Majdi would say to me, "OK Lesley, let's go" Once outside he would relate to me the story, common to all these visits that because I was a foreigner the renters were asking top dollar for rent on the assumption that I earned the same salary as those who worked for the UN.

Eventually I found an excellent three- bedroom flat at the bottom of the hill to Bet Jala opposite an olive grove. The owners were aunt and uncle to one of my Palestinian colleagues and had both been educated in Europe. Even then I had to negotiate hard to keep the price down to what I could afford. I could add to the price what it cost me to move out of my old flat in terms of redecorating and cleaning, but that is another story.

How far is it to Bethlehem?

How far is it to Bethlehem?

How far is it to Bethlehem?

How far is it to Bethlehem?

How far is it to Bethlehem?

How far is it to Bethlehem?

How far is it to Bethlehem?

At the Hairdressers

"Why do you think she is here?"

"What, you mean, in this salon?"

"No. Why is she here in Palestine?"

This conversation was going on around me as I sat in Lourice's Hair Salon in Bethlehem, waiting for her to finish back combing the beautiful blue-black tresses of my neighbour, Mimi, who was attending a formal dinner at the Latin Partiarchate that evening with her husband.

When the last puff of hair spray had settled and the last flick of Lourice's comb stopped, she rose out the chair like Venus emerging from the sea. After paying what was due, she waved at me saying, "ciao, Lesley, see you later," and scattered dazzling smiles to all the other ladies present.

This provoked another round of discussion about the foreigner in their midst.

"She must be invited to the dinner too."

"I wonder how she knows the Patriarch. She is not even Catholic."

As I was invited to sit on the throne, Lourice grinned at me and began to speak in English, another source of wonder and topic of conversation in the salon.

"Shall I tell them that you can understand what they are saying? They all think you don't speak Arabic."

"No, don't spoil their fun. Besides you would spoil my fun too. I do enjoy listening to what they have to say about me."

She smiled enigmatically at those waiting to be seen and regaled them with blatantly untrue and slightly risqué tales of my life in England which fascinated these dear ladies, wearing their traditional Arab dresses and holding their head scarves in their laps ready to receive their annual cropping before the feast. I came to Lourice when my hair needed cutting because she was the aunt of my secretary and that is how you did things in Bethlehem.

All recommendations came by word of mouth via a brother, a cousin, or an uncle, of which there seemed an endless supply. I only had to open my mouth and say I needed new cushions for my sofa, and behold, somebody had a relative with a shop down near Deheisha Refugee Camp. They would take me at the end of the day.

At the opposite end of the spectrum, my presence was always noted at funeral gatherings. Obviously, I was different because I didn't wear a long thobe and headscarf. It was not expected that foreign women would be happy to sit with Palestinian women as they mourned the death of their relatives or neighbours. But of course, the deceased was Amjad, the brother of my friend Majdi. He had died of leukemia.

I walked into a room full of women of all ages, gently weeping as they listened to a reading from the Quran. Fortunately, it was only about five minutes that my presence was the subject of speculation as I picked up phrases I recognized.

"Who is she? Why is she here?" I sat quietly in a corner until Firyal, Majdi's sister, entered. She came over to me and kissed me on both cheeks.

I was amazed to hear that Majdi would be taking Amjad's wife and children into his own house. I knew how much it cost him to send his own boys to the Freres School and tried to calculate how much that cost would now increase and was reminded of the Old Testament Levitical laws about family responsibility for orphans and widows.

I had a lump in my throat as I realized then that Palestinian women's obsession with the lives of foreign women was because they thought we lived different lives. When we joined in everyday activities in their society, they saw we were just like them.

A Very Special Woman

Crying does not indicate you are weak. Since that first cry of a child being born; it has always been a sign that you are alive. That is good to know. I always feel better after a good cry, although British people are supposed to be stoical. Well, that is how the rest of the world thinks of us.

My mind goes back to the evening when I heard a rumour about the lovely woman, Zahera, on my staff, who came from a village outside Hebron. It was being said that she had been killed in a car accident on her way home from university. She had not been alone in the car but was accompanied by her two-year old son. We waited with dread for this to be confirmed or denied. Sadly, it was the former. The whole department went into deep depression and students and colleagues spent hours weeping and telling stories about her.

In the Middle East, funerals usually take place within 24 hours, followed by four days of mourning. A group of us piled into the university minibus and the men left us women at the house designated for our mourning and left us to drive on to the men's place of mourning.

As I entered the house with Dr Jacqueline, our Palestinian Christian Dean, I realized I was the only foreigner present, and the room was filled with women of all ages from the village, quietly weeping and comforting each other. Zahera's sister-in-law came towards me and threw her arms round my neck, whispering "*Habibti, Zahera rahat* -My dear, Zahera has left us" I couldn't manage to express any words in English or Arabic so just hugged her close and found myself in the centre of a group hug.

Sitting with this community of women I listened to the rhythmic sound of Koranic readings, I wondered how Yasser was going to cope with a two-year old with a broken leg and older children fretting for their mother.

I remembered his pride in his wife who had a degree from Leipzig, in what was then East Germany, and how he had welcomed us foreigners into his house, cooking *kebabs and qatief*, Ramadan sweets, on the little stove in the centre of the living area. How they had provided me with a bed instead of a mattress on the floor when I stayed overnight with them.

Dr Jaqueline leaned over to me, "I need to tell you what these women are saying. Zahera was a special person in this community, someone they all looked up to."

It reminded me of being in Yasser and Zahera's house when a neighbour came to ask Zahera to administer an injection that had been prescribed by a doctor in one of the local hospitals. I had looked at my colleague and wondered where she had learnt to give injections, not something that was part of my physiotherapy curriculum that I could remember. Seeing my look of surprise, she whispered, "I am the only person in the village with medical training, so I had to learn how to do it."

As I looked round at this huge crowd of women genuinely shocked by the death of one of their own, I realized that my friend's loss to this community was much more even than her loss to the university. This was the point at which my British resolve crumbled, and I found myself crying for my wonderful friend, glad to be part of this amazing community of strong women who were not afraid to show that they cared.

So Much Depends Upon

Moishe lives in Hebron. He is 22 years old and is doing his national service in the Israeli Defence Force. His parents made *alyah* to Israel in 1937 from Germany, just ahead of Hitler and the Holocaust. He hopes that his national service record will earn him enough points to be able to study physiotherapy at Tel Aviv University when he leaves the military.

Musa lives in Hebron. He is 22 years old and is a first-year student at Bethlehem University studying physiotherapy after being in an Israeli jail for throwing stones at soldiers. His parents and grandparents have lived in the Old City as long as they can remember and have the title deeds to their house from Ottoman times.

Moishe and his family are Orthodox Jews and live in a Jewish enclave in the centre of Hebron. His community is constantly protected by soldiers of the IDF. He belongs to the ultra-right politico/religious party headed up by Rabbi Meir Kahane because he believes that Bibi Netanyahu doesn't.do enough to support the settlers in the West Bank.

Musa and his family are Sunni Muslims. They are among the few families to still live in the Old City, uncomfortably close to the Israeli settlers. He was a member of the Palestine Liberation Organisation but became disillusioned with Yasser Arafat's government. This led to him becoming a member of Hamas.

These two men met when Moishe was on duty at a checkpoint from Hebron to Bethlehem and Musa was trying to get to the Dome of the Rock for Friday prayers.

Musa saw a tall fair haired Semitic looking man in crumpled military uniform with a Kalashnikov over his shoulder and wearing a black skull cap on his head.

Moishe saw a tall dark- haired Semitic looking man dressed in a pristine white gallabiyah and a small white knitted skull cap on his head, looking angry and scared.

132

Two hours later they were both still there in the heat of the late morning, thirsty and irritated. They were trying to communicate in a combination of Arabic and Hebrew with a smattering of English when they reached an impasse in conversation.

Moishe was trying to follow his orders to detain young Palestinian Muslim men supposedly heading to Friday prayers but with possible ulterior motives.

Musa was trying to reign in his anger at Israelis sufficiently to make his case for entering Jerusalem with the appropriate permission. He was angry that someone of another religion could prevent him praying at the Al Aksar Mosque.

Each of them felt that they were right, and the other person was wrong.

Each of them carried with them their entire national history in their heart and a huge prejudice on their shoulders based on rumour and lack of understanding of the other.

So much depends on your background – soldier or so-called terrorist.

So much depends on your history - Jewish or Muslim, Israeli or Palestinian.

So much depends on your family experience – settler or resident.

So much depends on your perspective.

Just Smile

"Wasn't that lucky?" How many times have I said that? Do I really believe in luck? Or do I think that what appears to be luck is possibly something more?

I will let you decide after I share my story.

I had been in Nablus for a week, organising a continuing education course and was now driving to visit friends on the other side of the Green Line. I had never crossed the border at this point before, so it was all unknown and I was quite apprehensive. To get from the West Bank into Israel proper I had to negotiate a checkpoint, smile, and say "*Shalom*" to the Israeli soldiers on duty there.

Having behaved itself all week, as I drove the car up the last hill before the border, the steering wheel started to vibrate and on getting out I found I had a puncture. This posed me with a huge dilemma as I had stopped just too far on the Palestinian side of the border for the Israeli soldiers to feel comfortable coming to help me. On the other hand, I was too close to the checkpoint for any Palestinian driver to feel safe stopping either.

Not knowing quite what to do, I waited in hope for someone from either side to help me. During the next fifteen minutes I was disappointed by drivers, going in both directions, who not only did not stop, but speeded up as they passed. I felt a bit like the man in the parable who was attacked on the road from Jerusalem to Jericho. Everybody passed by on the other side. No sign of a good Samaritan.

Finally, a driver coming up the hill from Nablus slowed down, opened his door, and offered to change the wheel. I breathed a sigh of relief. Here was my good Samaritan, ironically on his home ground in Samaria.

At this point, the soldiers at the checkpoint became very interested in both of us. "Don't worry" my rescuer whispered and shouted in Hebrew, waving his arm towards the checkpoint, and walking over to speak with them. This seemed to restore peace and he quickly changed the wheel, all the while chatting to me in English. His interest in my activities was explained when he admitted he was a nurse at Rafidia Hospital in Nablus but couldn't understand why I was crossing the border into Israel at this point. I explained that the friends I was going to visit lived just over the border at Ra'anana and it was much quicker to cross here than go back south and travel up through Jerusalem and Tel Aviv. He was much impressed that I worked with Palestinians and had Israeli friends.

My thanks were heartfelt, and I added, "how come you were brave enough to stop?" He explained that he lived and worked in Nablus but had a brother living in Taybeh, an Arab village on the Israeli side of the Green Line. He was on his way there to celebrate the christening of his nephew the next day and that he was one of the godfathers to the boy. I wished him a good weekend with his family and drove off, passing the soldiers with a cheery wave.

Later at dinner that evening, with my Israeli friends I recounted the story of my good Samaritan friend. "Wasn't that lucky he had family on both sides?" they responded. Was it lucky I wondered or was it providential? Is that how the man on the road from Jerusalem to Jericho felt when he was safely installed at an inn? Or was he just glad to be alive?

Living the Dream!

"Nothing ventured, nothing gained," they say, don't they? So here I am on my way to Gaza. I have been to Gaza many times before but have always been able to leave when I wanted. This time I was going to stay; I had taken a job with the United Nations and wasn't entirely sure what I had let myself in for.

They gave me a UN car which immediately made me the target of every Palestinian and Israeli man, especially inside Gaza. Previously I had driven a car with Save the Children Fund emblazoned everywhere and a flurry of large red crosses attached to every visible surface. This was supposed to prevent Palestinian boys throwing stones at me, thinking I was an Israeli settler. It didn't always work if someone had a grudge against the Red Cross. Nor was it helpful when I lost my way in West Jerusalem and found myself in Meir She'arim, the ultra-orthodox Jewish district.

The UN, in the specific form of United Nations Relief and Works Agency (UNRWA) was simultaneously despised and tolerated in Gaza. All five refugee camps in Gaza were administered by UNRWA; food, schooling and health was provided and taken advantage of. Refugees didn't really want such assistance, but relied on it as a right, although they still thought of themselves as coming from the villages from which they had fled in 1948.

The three British staff (programme director, English teacher and myself) lived "over the shop" as it were; upstairs from the Nursing College in self-contained flats. I had a bedroom, a sitting room and a kitchen, all with ceiling fans which just moved around the hot air. The best part was a wide balcony where we could sit out and drink red wine in the early evening when all the students and local staff had gone home. The only disadvantage to this arrangement was the Baptist missionaries who also lived at this level in the next block, and they looked askance at our drinking alcohol.

I didn't discover until months later when visiting patients in a second-floor ward of the nearby Baptist Hospital that our antics caused great hilarity to the more mobile patients who could see across to our balcony. I breathed a sigh of relief that I had never attempted to sunbathe on the balcony.

I soon found out there was not much "social life" in Gaza. We were sometimes invited to eat dinner with local colleagues where one sat cross-legged on the floor, sometimes with a cushion behind you, so you could lean against a wall. The visit of a foreigner meant that all the extended family, plus a fair sprinkling of neighbours, came by to watch us struggling with unfamiliar food, eaten without the aid of utensils.

We soon tired of cooking for each other, and the only other option was the UN Gaza Strip Club. Initially a visit there was a breath of fresh air with the opportunity to speak English without careful consideration of one's vocabulary and delivered at normal speed. It was a gathering of many nations, as all those working in the Strip congregated to eat western food and drink at the bar. The only problem was that the same people were there every night and conversation soon became boring and repetitious.

Once one had watched all the films available in the library, worked your way through the limited menu and sampled all the different gins at the bar, the only thing left to do was buy all your family members tee shirts stamped with The Gaza Strip Club. Still – it was only a six- month contract; surely, I could survive that?

Student Strike

"The physiotherapy students have gone on strike!" greeted me as I walked through the main gate of the university. I was head of the new occupational therapy (OT) programme, but my students took classes with the physio students. My blood pressure went up as I thought of all the difficulties we had already faced and how they would now increase.

My students swirled around me uttering frightened cries and complaints, all trying to get my attention at the same time. The physio students stood on the other side of the courtyard, arms crossed, scowling, and making threats. What had happened? On Friday when we left for the weekend everyone was friendly and both groups of students wished me a happy weekend.

Pushing my way through the press of students from other faculties now as word had gone round about the strike, I made my way down the corridor to the office of my dean. Her secretary squeezed my hand sympathetically and quickly ushered me into her boss's office. There I found my colleague, who was heading up the physio course, sipping Arabic coffee and looking complacent and triumphant. Eventually my mind cleared enough to realise that he had told the physio students that the standard of their education would go down and that they would not be recognized as professionals internationally if they took classes with the OT students.

This was not true, of course, but it was believed at the university by staff and students, consultation by gossip being a way of life in Palestine. This situation was the latest outcome of the Academic Vice President's decision to make Mohammed Acting Head of Physiotherapy. He did love "acting", it was so much more real to him than life.

"What are we going to do, Lesley?" Dr Jaqueline had not had to deal with a situation like this before. "The Academic Board supports you, but the Student Council want you to appear before them and answer these charges."

Fortunately, by this time, Bethlehem University was connected to the internet. I asked for twenty-four hours to consult with colleagues in other countries and spent the next twelve hours glued to a computer. I emailed Sarah, who had been the external educational evaluator of a similar programme in Southampton; she confirmed that their graduates had been able to register after graduation with both the Physiotherapy and Occupational Therapy Associations.

This was good but I did not think somehow that experience in the UK would be enough to sway things in my favour, so I contacted the World Confederation of Physiotherapy and the World Federation of Occupational Therapy who confirmed my findings. I was now armed with evidence to convince the Student Council and mad enough to take on all comers.

Six senior students invited me to their office, all men, of course, and started to grill me. I sat directly in front of them, determined not to be intimidated clutching my file of papers. As I presented my case, I gradually saw a change come over their faces and their deportment became less confrontational. At the end of the meeting one young man, majoring in English Literature, smiled, "I wish that my programme leader was as caring of his students as you are. I think I might switch to rehabilitation myself." I smiled back with relief but prayed he wouldn't change majors.

The strike was over, thank goodness, I thought. Not quite, some of the more militant male physio students maintained that nothing had changed. The Vice Chancellor got involved at this point advising Mohammed to resign before he was brought before the Academic Council, which would probably lead to dismissal.

Such a mess, all the result of appointing someone to an "Acting" position. Possession is nine tenths of the law here.

Wait

"Let me explain why I don't speak much Hebrew," I said to the middle-aged Jewish lady with the very fetching wig who had accosted me at the bar mitzvah of my friend's son.

She looked at me from under her brows, "I don't understand. If you have been in this country for ten years, why didn't you learn Hebrew?" I tried to marshal my thoughts quickly before I admitted that I was working and living in Bethlehem in the West Bank with Palestinians. As I found the words to say what I wanted she said, "oh you mean Judea and Samaria. How unusual?"

I wondered why she thought it unusual and then realised that she had probably never met any of the international aid workers who volunteered for various charities in the West Bank. She lived in Tel Aviv and probably had never met an Israeli Arab, let alone a Palestinian.

"Well, I still don't understand why you don't know more Hebrew."

I tried to explain that if I needed to speak any other language it was Arabic as this was the language my students and colleagues spoke. However, most of my colleagues had done their higher education abroad so many could speak English and other European languages too. Those who had been born in Israel proper also spoke Hebrew.

"I do know a little Hebrew," and admitted that the bar mitzvah boy and his sister had taught me what Hebrew I knew.

"But you must have to speak Hebrew to some people when you visit Jackie?"

Again I had to explain that most of Jackie's friends and the people I met when I shopped in Jerusalem spoke much better English than me. She was not impressed to learn that I went to Arabic classes either.

"You must be very lazy if you have been in this country for ten years and never bothered to learn the main language."

I thought of all the hours I spent writing curricula suitable for educating therapists to meet the needs of the Palestinian population but couldn't face having to explain why I didn't just teach the same in Bethlehem as I had in Bradford. I did manage to smile sweetly and plead lack of time because of preparing teaching notes and marking student assignments.

"Well surely you have done all this before. You don't need to make a lot of changes."

I wondered how she would feel if the teachers of her grandchildren had admitted recycling notes and exams ad nauseum.

Her final volley was, "I don't know why you needed to work in an Arab university. What is wrong with our Israeli universities? Why didn't you work there?" I hastened to assure her that Israeli universities were very good and didn't need people like me.

At this point Jackie came back to rescue me. I breathed a sigh of relief and said "Please don't leave me alone with that woman, I feel like I have been interviewed for a job."

Panic

"I can't find it!" I panicked when I couldn't find my handbag. It was not in my backpack, and I did not remember seeing it since the weaving factory in Beersheva. My rummaging through my backpack had alerted my friends that somethings was wrong, "look again it must be there."

It wasn't found even after we had searched all our bags, under the seats of the car and in the boot. What was I going to do? The bag contained my passport and credit cards, in addition to a substantial amount of money in dollars and pounds.

We retraced our steps to shops we had visited as my blood pressure continued to rise despite my deep breathing and attempted relaxation techniques. No success! So, what next?

Our Palestinian friend, Bassam, finally said, "OK let's go back to the chicken place in Hebron where we had lunch." The drive back was in the dark as dusk comes suddenly in the Middle East and all the traffic seemed to be travelling in our direction causing hold ups and horn blowing. Eventually we arrived back at the café to find that the man who had served us had finished his shift and his replacement kept shaking his head in answer to Bassam's questions in Arabic. We insisted he call his absent colleague and I watched as he spoke and shrugged his shoulders and finally unearthed my bag from under a pile of towels behind the counter.

With relief I noticed my passport and credit cards intact, but all my cash had disappeared. When he heard this Bassam said to the young man and the gradually increasing crowd of interested spectators come to see the foreigner's discomfort, "we will have to call the police."

"The nearest police station is miles away," they chorused. "We will find them wherever the police station is." Bassam informed them looking very serious. "They will be able to see who stole the bag from the security camera outside."

Though they told us the camera was not working, we saw it was and that the boys were beginning to get worried. Bassam told them that if the money was returned immediately, we would not inform the police. At this point the young man behind the counter dashed outside and quickly returned with my dollars in his open hand which I took. He then offered me his wallet and on opening it I found my sterling inside and transferred it to my wallet. Still looking very determined, but with my blood pressure now under control we walked out to our car.

Jo, who had stayed in the car during these transactions, had watched a white car drive up and down the street, from which the money and wallet eventually had appeared. I thanked Bassam profusely and named him my knight in shining armour. He said, "I knew my strategy would work because I know my people".

A Dangerous Monster Threatens the Community

A dangerous monster threatens the community, we are told. We must stay at home to prevent the monster spreading from house to house. My grandfather sits on the balcony drinking his morning coffee and muses on events past and present. He would normally drink his coffee with his friends down at the local café but, of course, he cannot, because we are confined to home. He has got to the age when past and present intertwine so closely that it is difficult sometimes to work out to what he is referring.

"This reminds me of the curfews the Israelis placed on us during the First Intifada. You were not allowed to leave the house then or you might be shot. Only the women were allowed out for an hour each day to buy fresh bread," he mutters, half to himself, but also to remind me that we have met this monster before.

"So how did you get through the experience last time *Teta*?" I ask, partly to keep him occupied while my mother makes breakfast, and partly because I can't remember the curfews he mentions, I was just a baby.

"We would go to the window, checking first there were no Israeli soldiers around and would whistle across to the neighbours, who would come to their window and shout greetings to us."

"We can still do that today, *Teta*, I can open the window and call to Abu Daud so you can talk with him" "So you can *habibi,* unfortunately my hearing is not so good now, so he needs to shout louder."

"Remember we can Skype him and you can see him and talk to him on the laptop. Surely that is better than shouting."

Teta smiles at me as he says, "thank God for such modern means of communication. But speaking to my neighbour on a screen is not as much fun as leaning out of the window."

He sighs again more deeply, "then of course we were all here in this house. It was a bit cramped but were all together to face the monster. This time, Nicola is in America and Manar is in England, so far away from home, among strangers when they should be with their family."

"When you talk to them on Skype they look well, and Immi says they look healthy."

"Yes, but they should be here where I can take care of them" Nothing can persuade him that his absent children and grandchildren can look after themselves.

His face takes on an even greater sadness when he remembers his grandson, Butros, who is in an Israeli prison, convicted of throwing stones at soldiers. We have heard nothing from him for weeks and no-one is allowed to visit him. I can usually find something to say to my *Teta* to cheer him up, that is one of my jobs in the family. However, today there is nothing I can say about this and nothing I can do except squeeze his hand.

The monster showed up just after midnight. As they do. I was awakened by my mother, "munther, wake up. Your grandfather is burning up and he can't breathe. We need to get him to hospital."

I dressed quickly and went to Tata's room. His breathing was laboured and he kept coughing. The whole family crowded round. My training as a paramedic kicked in and I said "Everybody out but me and Immi. Go into your own room and stay there."

I told my mother "Wash your hands and don't get too close to the bed. I need to get my kit out of the ambulance."

Thank God that I had been allowed to park the van outside my house. I quickly rummaged inside and got surgical gloves and masks which Immi and I put on. I managed to shout to my brother to phone the government hospital down in Bethlehem.

"They can't take *Teta* as they have no beds. They suggest we phone the Bethlehem Arab Society to see how they are placed."

"Do it!" I yelled as I tried to persuade my grandfather to drink some water.

He was becoming more confused by the minute telling me that I must not let any soldiers into the house. "It will be ok. They won't come tonight." I whispered. Receiving a message from my brother that we could take Tata up the hill, my mother and I cradled him in a blanket and carried him out to the ambulance. I drove up the hill like a maniac. Fortunately, there was no other traffic as I took the one-way street going the wrong way past the Orthodox Church of St Nicolas.

Getting into the hospital was not easy. We had to push through the crowd of people waiting for news of their relatives admitted there over the last six hours. Eventually my Tata was given a bed in the paediatric ward (emptied of children) as it was the only ward with empty beds. We waited for a doctor to appear and after half an hour a tired young man in rumpled scrubs arrived and started his examination. He looked over at me and gently shook his head. Somehow, I didn't think this was going to end well. This monster would not go away.

A Brief History of Betrayal

He badly needed the job. Since the Uprising and his return home his savings were slowly dwindling. He saw the advert in the newspaper and thought, "I could do that! I don't think many local people could do it as well as me." At the interview he was surprised that three other men applied. Did they think they could do the job as well as him? Not a chance.

He took part in the interview, the group discussion and other selection activities with his tongue in his cheek. If this is what these crazy foreigners thought would help them decide who was best, then he would play the game. It was obvious he was well ahead of all the others, and he had no doubt he would be chosen. In the end they chose two people and he found himself working with a man he didn't like, who had been a student with him in Egypt.

Of course, he didn't have a problem working for a boss who was female. As long as she was the head of department, he would be a good boy, but just wait until he was in charge. Things would change then. He faithfully studied all the new student-centred philosophies introduced from the west and even did his best to use some of them in his classes. However, his best move was when he married the American administrator, and she gained him access to a whole new world.

His big chance came when his boss went back home for a sabbatical. When the university authorities offered him the Acting Head position, he saw this as his way to the top. After all acting could easily become permanent and in his case it did.

The story moves on to a time when a new course was to be offered and the previous head came back to run it. The sponsors wanted the two courses to have some modules in common, but Mohammed saw this as an invasion of his territory and dug his heels in. He provoked a student strike telling the students, "taking classes with students from this new course will lower the standard of our course."

Sadly, the university backed the foreigner, so he felt he had to resign, hoping that the university would not accept his decision. His next trick was to get one of the students to send an anonymous threatening letter to his British colleague.

She was told, "you are no more welcome in this country. You should leave at once." Instead of frightening her, it made her angry and the university and local police provided protection.

Years later, now working in the USA, he heard that his ex-boss was also now home. He was horrified that she would burst his balloon and spread information about his activities in his home country. He wondered if it had all been worth it. Instead of being a respected head of department in the most reputable university in his home country, revered by his peers and adored by his students, he was one member of a large team of teachers in an American university, where very few people know him. Yes, he could hide there, and his salary was secure but the brilliant future he had dreamed of had not materialized.

A Most Unusual Angel

He did not look like anyone special at all. Nothing to make you think he might be other than a very ordinary man. He barely came up to my shoulder and was almost as broad as he was long. Obviously not a Palestinian Arab, despite his sallow complexion, unruly black hair and bushy black eyebrows. You certainly might be concerned if you met him on a dark night.

I was trying to leave Gaza and had discovered that the Israeli authorities had closed the border, and no-one seemed to know when, or if, it would reopen. This was the final straw. Getting in had been hard enough. Leaving Israel hadn't been a problem, if you discounted the massive border post with its signs in Hebrew, its automatic exit gates controlled by flashing red and green lights. Lugging two cases full of books did not help, especially when trying to go through turn-style gates, that required a special art.

I had permission to leave Israel and the young soldier, who haled originally from Manchester, stamped my passport with a flourish and wished me a nice day in a tone that implied that such a day was not possible in a place like Gaza. What I did not know, neither did my colleague Mohammed, as it turned out, I also needed permission from the Hamas administration to enter Gaza. All the contents of my luggage were deftly and efficiently, turned over by a very pleasant policewoman and then we waited and waited and waited.

As was his custom, Mohammed told me not to worry. It would all get sorted out and he proceeded to walk up and down bellowing into his mobile phone as he spoke with all his important contacts. A man in a black leather jacket, who I assumed was a border guard, asked me why "my fixer" had not arranged the necessary permission. Eventually I was allowed in, on the understanding that I would complete the appropriate form, with photo, retrospectively.

My five-day visit passed, as I visited all my friends and old colleagues, coping with the power cuts and talking for hours by candlelight whilst eating mountains of rice and various fish and meat dishes and drinking copious amounts of coca cola. In between all this partying we traipsed from one government office to another to purchase the appropriate form, then adding a photo to it, at the official photo booth and finally getting another Hamas official stamp on it. Now I was legal and perhaps they would let me out when my visit ended.

I was on my way out of this open- air prison, but the border was closed. Sighing deeply, I sat down next to this ordinary man, who said to me very confidently "Don't worry. They will open the gates quite soon" I wondered at his confidence until he told me he did this trip once a week. Looking more closely at this little man in his heavy black coat I noticed his clerical collar and wondered what he had been doing in Gaza. He regaled me with stories of his small Catholic congregation and their challenges in living in such a strict Islamic society until the crowd began to move forward and we realized that the border was open.

That was when the nightmare really began. Palestinian porters almost shoveled us into a large room where they were directed in their work by Israeli soldiers up on a building high above us, shouting in Hebrew. I began to panic as I did not know what to expect. Father Pablo, as I now knew his name, saw my eyes widen and he patted my arm, "don't worry, we need to open our cases and put them on that carousel over there. The only thing you can hang on to is your passport and your wallet as you pass through that Xray machine and hold your arms up."

In one of my cases I had four litres of honey that relatives in Gaza had sent to their son in England. I was sure the Israelis were going to confiscate it. As it happened, only one container was opened, and I managed to get the other three jars safely back to the UK. Coming out into the cool early evening air my heart rate began to return to its usual level and I looked again at this man who looked so ordinary.

"Thank you so much, Father Pablo. I wouldn't have coped without you."

He shrugged modestly and smiled sympathetically. I had heard other people say that they had met angels and had not believed their stories, but now I couldn't sneer at anyone ever again. I had met my own little South American angel.

How Does it Feel to be Followed?

I found out one wet day in November when I opened the door to my office. There on the floor was an A4 sheet of white paper. I picked it up and placed it on my desk while I divested myself of my waterproofs. After eight years I had finally got used to the winter downpours. No longer surprised by their ferocity I shook myself down and put the kettle on for a cup of coffee.

Now looking at the sheet of paper I saw typed in badly phrased English, "Lesly Dawson. You are no longer welcome in this country. It is not safe for you to stay. You should leave immediately."

This should have made me afraid, but it just made me angry. How dare anyone say this to me. After all this time I considered myself half Palestinian. Who would write this?

If it was a student, he had been encouraged in this by someone else. I knew it was a "he". In fact, I knew which "he" it was. I remembered the torn-up exam paper I had found trampled in the mud the previous day. The owner had been so incensed by the grade he had received that he didn't want to keep it.

I also knew which "he" had encouraged the student to write this. My Palestinian colleague was flexing his academic muscles. He had disagreed violently with my decision to teach physiotherapy and occupational therapy students together in some classes and this was his revenge.

I picked up the phone and dialed the number for the Academic Vice President's office, "*Sabahel kher Hannah, kif halik*? I need to speak with Dr Manno urgently." Hannah would call me when he was free. An hour later I sat in his office drinking Arabic coffee. He had even remembered that I drank it without sugar. "OK Lesley, what is the problem? You never ask to see me with so much urgency."

I passed the communication to him. As he read it his eyes widened and his face became florid. I could almost see his blood pressure rising.

"This is disgraceful. You are a valued member of staff." He looked up at me "Has this upset you? We don't want to lose you."

"Who would do this?" I could hardly speak through my anger as I told him my suspicions which I couldn't prove.

He nodded wisely and picked up the phone. The next thing I knew was the arrival of a man dressed in police uniform. He was introduced as Major Khaled, the head of security in Bethlehem.

"Don't worry *Doctora*. We will send a police car every few hours to patrol the street where you live. This is my phone number if you need to call, use it day or night."

My safety on campus was assured by the university's own security staff who I knew well and exchanged greetings with each morning. I began to feel that I was being followed around as I went from class to class but instead of worrying me, it made me feel safe.

Not What I Wanted at All

So that was that. They had accepted my resignation. Not what I had wanted at all. That dratted foreigner had won. Now what was I going to do? It had all started so well. She had been granted a semester sabbatical to analyse the data for her thesis in the UK. At the time I was abroad myself, with my wife and my baby daughter in Dublin. I had just written to the Academic Vice President asking for permission to extend our stay there, so I could upgrade from Master to Doctorate level study. In the UK this is not an unusual request, but the AVP being American didn't understand what was going on and suspected I was trying to get out of returning to Nablus.

The absent programme head had arranged for teaching to continue in her absence and those teachers still in Nablus were to each take on specific responsibilities. Despite this the AVP's email to me had a slight triumph in its tail. He was ordering me back to the university to take over as Acting Programme Head.

My initial reaction to his email was anger and frustration. How could I get ahead of my colleagues if I didn't have a PhD. This was the gold star that was recognized by my university and there was no way that a Masters' degree (although considered a silver star) would suffice to get me where I wanted to be. As I digested the news that I could not move higher with my studies, I drank gallons of Arabic coffee and smoked endless cigarettes, much to the disgust of my wife and the distress of my small daughter. I even indulged in the forbidden and got through a few bottles of Irish whiskey.

As I began to calm down my wife pointed out that I had ignored the end of the email. Three months as Acting Programme Head would install me back into the university hierarchy and maybe offer the possibility for it to become permanent.

So we returned home and took up my new post.

Ignoring the "Acting" part of my title I began to make the changes I had always wanted. On her return, my previous boss was supposed to act as my adviser, but I didn't want to be advised. She eventually took the hint and moved to Gaza to a job in a Nursing College there.

Called to a meeting in the Vice Chancellor's office I discovered that a group of Norwegian occupational therapists wanted to sponsor a degree in that profession, alongside our programme.

"After all there are many things in common, so it would make sense to offer both physiotherapy and occupational therapy," I smiled politely, vowing to have nothing to do with this project. It was with horror that I gradually realized that the headship of this OT programme had been offered to my ex-boss. She was returning to get in my way again.

Because the Norwegians held the purse strings, they were calling the tune. They suggested that the two groups of students should take modules in subjects such as anatomy and physiology and social sciences together. My heart sank; I had little experience of this other profession and didn't want to share anything with them. The Norwegians got their way, and the first group of OT students was selected. Early shared classes got underway, much against my better judgement.

Not being happy with this situation I began to drop hints about the standard of the OT profession and how sharing with them would lower the standard of our qualification. Thus began a rumble of disquiet among the physiotherapists, especially the men who were very status conscious. All this developed into a strike of my students and as the two groups were sharing this module, it also affected the OT students. The university was in uproar, especially as I had informed the AVP that unless the two programmes were separated, I would resign.

Who has the Last Word?

"Dr Lesley, Can I speak to you about my assignment?"

"Of course. What about your essay?"

"Forgive me, but I think you might have made a mistake."

"Really. What mistake have I made?"

"Well, maybe not a mistake but would you please consider remarking my assignment. I think I should have a higher mark."

This conversation took place outside my office after I had returned the assignment papers to the students. Rami was not happy with his grade. It was too low and what was more important to him, it would lower his Grade Point Average. He needed a high GPA as he wanted to get a scholarship to study in the USA.

This was not the first time he and I had had a disagreement over the value of his written work. The previous semester I had been out to dinner with friends at the Shepard Hotel. Foreigners were usually well looked after there, especially if they thought you were American and would leave a large tip. However, this time it was a bit over the top. After taking our order the waiter sidled up to me so no one else could hear our conversation. Here we go, I thought, he wants to get a place for his son, nephew, cousin in the next physiotherapy intake. I sighed as I turned to him with my brightest smile plastered on my face.

"*Doctora,* you know that my nephew, Rami, is hoping for a scholarship to Lewis University in Chicago?"

"Yes?"

"He is a poor refugee and needs high grades from you."

At this he nodded his head in the direction of the kitchen and lo and behold, Rami walked towards us bearing a large tray on which a beautiful cream cake glistened in the lamp light. We had certainly not ordered that.

"We would like to present this dessert to you and your friends, as a gift from us."

"That is very kind of you, but we don't deserve it."

"Oh, but you do deserve it. You are a very kind lady."

I explained to my surprised guests just exactly what this was – a bribe to ensure his nephew got good grades in his next assignment. It probably also meant that the boy hadn't done the work and was hoping I would overlook his poor performance.

Accepting a slice of the cake would imply an understanding of what I had to do. Refusing it, in this culture, was also not an option. What a mess. I couldn't come to this restaurant ever again.

Rami sat outside my office, looking very sorry for himself all morning. I saw him as I walked down the corridor from my class. I was in desperate need of a cup of coffee before I could deal with this.

What could I say that would convince him that I was not going to remark his essay on the causes of poliomyelitis?

Having gulped down half a cup of terrible instant coffee, I had no excuses left. I went over for what seemed like the hundredth time the reasons he had scored such low marks, gently explaining to him again that students submitted work based on their studies and teachers graded what they found in the work, based on their professional integrity. This was something I had never expected to have to say to any student but there it was out in the open.

I did consider taking him into my office and showing hm the poster an American colleague had given me, 'Which part of the word No do you not understand?' I rejected this idea as too subtle for the boy in front of me.

In the end I said, "*Rami, khallas, bekafi* (stop, enough). Go to your next class," and surprisingly, he did.

Bit of a Bombshell Today

Part One

All the kids on our block, in fact in the whole of the town, marched down to the no -go area between us and Israel. You wouldn't have believed it. I usually hear whispers, especially from the boys, when they are intending to do something dangerous. That gives me time to tell their father who can try to knock some sense into them. I tell you they won't listen to me I am only their mother. This time we were all taken by surprise.

Up in Jerusalem, Donald Trump decided to move the US Embassy from Tel Aviv to Jerusalem. Surely, he knew what mayhem he would cause? Maybe he didn't care. We watched the early morning news on Israeli TV. We can get their programmes as we live near the border. I turned to my husband, "young men on both sides are going to be hurt as a result of this." He sighed and opened his mobile phone to call his medical team to ready their emergency equipment, but we didn't realise that the children would go as well as their elder brothers. Young women went, even the very religious ones, who cover their faces, which is unheard of.

My husband told me to stay at home, but he went off to the hospital to drive the ambulance out to the sand dunes and set up first aid tents. *Imm Walid* (my next door neigbour) and I decided that we would take food and drink to our families and see what would happen. I had heard that the Shabab, the young men, intended to march to the fence and cut through the barbed wire to enter Israel and reclaim our old villages. I wondered how they would fare armed only with slings and stones against the IDF with their tear gas and weapons.

I was worried as I saw the burning tires and excited young people edging closer and closer to the line of Israeli soldiers.

It was almost as though they thought it was a game daring each other to get the closest. At this point there was the sound of gun fire and I saw young men at the front fall down suddenly, howling that they had been hit in the leg. The paramedics, wearing their distinctive waist coats emblazoned with a large red crescent, rushed forward to carry the injured away to the first aid tents. I saw my son, Musa, doing his duty treating the injured and my heart swelled with pride at his bravery.

As the day wore on things got steadily worse as more young men and women were rushed from the fence to the first aid stations. As we peered through the smoke, *Imm Walid* gave a gasp and cried out "NO, please God, no". There in front of us, outlined against the sky on top of one of the sand dunes was her fourteen-year- old daughter Basma. The girl seemed unconcerned about the Israelis as she filled her pockets with stones for her brothers to put in their sling shots. I held my breath as she stood there, seemingly oblivious to her situation and prayed that no sniper on the other side had her in his sights. Sadly, her time was short. She fell to the ground and was rushed to the first aid tents and then to Al Ahli Hospital where she was pronounced dead, shot in the head.

As the sun went down there was a stream of young men, women and children returning to their home, faces streaming with the effects of tear gas and tears of frustration that they had failed in their attempt to cut through the fence.

Part Two

My platoon was called back from leave. There was a panic on. I was not pleased as I had arranged to take my younger brothers and sisters to the beach at Ashdod. My mother kissed me as I set off and whispered, "stay safe my son."

We found ourselves lined up along the fence we share with Gaza. We were told, "you snipers have instructions to shoot if you see anyone at all breach the barbed wire."

We looked at each other and some brave soul said, "even if they are unarmed Sarge?" He looked round at us all, "anyone who attempts to cut the wire is trying to invade us, so yes."

Trying to swallow our misgivings, we settled ourselves to await the onslaught. "Here they come" someone muttered. With that we saw a column of people walking down the road from Gaza as though they were out for a picnic. Looking through my binoculars I said" They look so young, some of them are just primary school kids."

"Never mind that," growled Amos, "remember what sarge said. They must not be allowed to enter Israel. Remember your kid brothers and sisters in school just over that hill."

"Oh my God," whimpered Boaz, "there are women and children coming towards us. How can I go home tonight and tell my mother that I shot a girl?" He was told to pull himself together and remember that girls were our enemies too.

Everything started to happen at once, old tires were set alight and the smoke irritated our eyes and interfered with our vision, the chanting of "Allah Akbar" got louder and stones began to whizz through the air, some of them reaching to where we were kneeling.

We started firing cannisters of tear gas and could see the effects from where we were deployed. I do not know who fired the first actual shot, but shots were fired and two teenagers who were closest to the fence went down with howls of rage and pain clutching their legs. By this time older men and women had joined the march and two men dressed as paramedics rushed forward with stretchers to take the boys to safety. We saw them carry the boys to large first aid tents that had been set up out of range of our shots.

The young boys kept coming closer, then moving back when they saw us look down our gun sights. It seemed like a game where they were daring each other to be the first to the wire. As more and more people gathered on the sand dunes inside the no-go area, things became more confusing.

We did receive instructions from spotters in the so-called War Room about who we should aim at. Nevertheless, I can't be sure where my bullets and tear gas went as I saw both males and females fall to the ground and then be rushed away.

Eventually we were stood down and another platoon took our place. We were told to stand by in case we were needed again, but as darkness fell, we were released to go home. We trudged wearily back to our headquarters, none of us able to string two words together. I don't know about anyone else, but I felt a heavy burden on my shoulders that had nothing to do with the gun I carried.

All our mothers showered us with kisses and cooked us our favourite food that night but those who were able to eat it probably didn't enjoy it as much as usual at the end of a shift.

Feeling at Home

The piece written for the university newsletter said it all.

"I arrived here eleven years ago, a Brit lost in Palestine. I leave as someone who considers herself half Palestinian and half British." This had not happened in a moment, but a series of moments, as slow and insidious, as the melting of the snow on Mount Hermon.

Remembering my early days, not knowing where to shop, how to ask for three bananas, where to get calor gas for the heater, that time was far behind. Taking spoken Arabic classes seemed a good idea, not realizing how difficult a language it was to learn. Smiling to myself, I remember thinking "I might now be able to do my shopping, understand my colleagues, visit the families of my students and write my given name in Arabic.

Unlike the alphabet used in western vocabulary, every letter is written in three different ways, at the beginning, in the middle or at the end of the word. This was in addition to everything seeming back to front, with writing going from right to left. Even if my vocabulary was limited and my writing non-existent, my accent was considered good enough to be Lebanese. However, the language problem could be easily overcome because most local teachers spoke English far better than I could speak Arabic.

A bigger issue was the attitude to time. An early meeting with a local social worker who had been educated in the UK made things clearer, "I know that you British are always on time and like other people to do the same, so here I am at the time we agreed."

Unfortunately, not many of her compatriots shared this attitude to time.

I cannot count the times, minutes, even hours, that were spent drinking hot chocolate on the terrace at the Notre Dame Café waiting for a meeting to start. Becoming gradually acclimatized culturally, I started to arrive on time but not to expect my visitors to be there for at least another half hour. Relative "at homeness" arrived when, not expecting meetings to begin on time, I arrived late myself and did not find that anyone thought badly of me for doing so.

However, this laisse faire attitude to time did not find its way into my classroom. There was no point in giving students a five-minute break, they would take fifteen and fifteen minutes would extend to thirty. Because I was British, I felt I could say "In my classroom we work on British time, so these are fifteen British minutes, not Palestinian minutes." Students gradually got used to what they saw as my rigid attitude to time and would joke with me about whose time we were keeping. Looking back, it did feel a bit imperialistic, but my excuse was that we had a lot to fit in to the timetable.

Great Expectations

The university was looking for two local therapists to shadow the two expatriate therapists who had started the training programme and so put an advert in the local papers. Four people applied for the jobs, all of them men. They all had to go through a rigorous selection process involving an interview in English, a group discussion, and a role play. They thought the foreigners were mad but badly wanted a job so played the game. Adnan and Islam got the jobs after the university had checked on their political and family backgrounds.

The plan was that these two would take over running the programme when the foreigners left. They were both from Gaza, one being a 1948 refugee from Israel and the other from an old well respected Gazan family. Both had trained in Egypt and practised their profession in the West Bank. They had high expectations about their future and so did the charity that funded the programme. Adnan rented a house in Jerusalem and Islam moved his family from Gaza to live in Bethlehem and enrolled his kids in schools there. They began to put down roots in and around Bethlehem.

Time went by and the situation in Israel and Palestine became more difficult. Whenever they went home to Gaza to visit the rest of the family it was not always easy to get out again as the checkpoints became stricter. A few times they were unable to get back to teach their classes and the university began to be concerned about their future there.

Eventually Adnan left Palestine with his Irish wife for work in the UK leaving Islam to carry the expectations of the funders. There were many times when he felt embarrassed that he had to phone his Head of School in Bethlehem and apologise that yet again he couldn't get out of Gaza. Eventually he could bear the embarrassment no longer and resigned. Gone were the hopes of the university to hand on responsibility to local therapists as was expected and in their place was a huge loss of face for the men concerned and for the reputation of the university. In addition to all this shame and embarrassment one of the foreign teachers had to stay on in post until the situation could be resolved.

The programme managed to continue somehow, and its students graduated and began to work in their profession, and some went abroad to do further study before they returned home. Others did not return at all. Twenty years later Islam is a well-respected therapy teacher in a university in Gaza and his graduates are thick on the ground there, providing a valuable service to that desperate place. Adnan now teaches in London but visits his family in Gaza from time to time. The original training programme in Bethlehem is now run by two of the first graduates who have gained experience abroad and returned home with their families. Nothing turned out as expected but in other ways expectations were met.

Forgive Me

Forgive me for being able to walk away unscathed, for being free, for having a passport that allows me to leave. These were my thoughts as the plane taxied across the airfield and began its ascent. I was leaving, I was going home.

I had lived among these wonderful, wounded people for so long, the place felt like home.

Yet I was leaving to go to a place that was supposed to be my home, a place where I no longer felt comfortable, where I felt a stranger. We had shared so much together, you shared so much with me. The laughter, the tears, the meals we had shared, the adventures, the anxiety, the passion for life. You took me to your hearts and into your families. Your mothers treated me as a sister, your fathers granted me their trust and respect.

I think that I will always feel guilty that I could leave and yet you smiled and wished me well when we said goodbye. I lost count of the farewell parties I attended and the gifts I had to find space for in my luggage. As I sit here with tears in my eyes, I think, 'don't be so stupid. You will be able to go back whenever you want. You will be able to send emails and photos. It is not as if you will never see people again.'

That thought cheers me up for a while as I pick up my plastic glass of dry white wine. I close my eyes and try to sleep as the flight is due into Gatwick at 8am tomorrow morning.

I remember the time I arranged for seventeen Palestinian students to go to the UK to experience life in a British hospital. There should have been two more, but they were refused exit permits because of their political activities. We arrived at Ben Gurion airport and immediately attracted every man and woman in the security services. With a tremor in my voice but trying to sound confident I said to the nearest man, "this is a letter from the Vice Chancellor of Bethlehem University for the Head of Security," I waved it just out of reach of the hands that tried to grab it until I saw an older man coming towards us.

Having allowed him to read the document, we followed him to the security area where each student's luggage was searched and then in pairs, they were taken away to be strip searched.

They had all been briefed about the security check and warned about the search. I stood and watched and encouraged them not to show their fear and hugged each one as they emerged from the search room, pale but smiling as they went to the plane.

Forgive me that I can't take you with me this time. That I leave you to deal with roadblocks, curfews, tear gas and possible interrogation. Despite all this I know that your spirit will overcome all this, the famed Palestinian, "*sumud*" or endurance will enable you to keep going and I will never forget what you have taught me.

Coming Home?

I came back to the UK after being away for eleven years to take up a job in a British university. Much to the surprise of family and friends in Yorkshire I elected to head south and settle in Eastbourne.

"Why Eastbourne?" they asked with raised eyebrows and disbelieving looks. "Isn't that the place where you spent six weeks when you were doing your teaching diploma back in the 1970's? I thought you couldn't get away fast enough then and now you are going back?"

Convinced that the Middle Eastern sun had done something permanent to my brain they changed the subject to talk about the poor goal scoring of Leeds United and the chances of the England Cricket Team winning the ashes.

When I left the UK, my professional training was a diploma, taught in schools located in teaching hospitals. I returned to a degree profession based in universities.

However, that wasn't the biggest challenge. In Bethlehem I had worked in an American-influenced university and had struggled to come to terms with professors and grade point averages and now I had to get used to calling courses, modules and programmes, courses.

Fortunately, there were a few non-Brits among the staff, but most had been living in the UK for some years, so weren't much help with my reverse culture shock. I found myself completely out of my depth and my learning curve was almost vertical. My colleagues had all specialized in discrete clinical areas such as musculoskeletal, neurological, paediatric and respiratory physiotherapy and couldn't understand when I said my specialism was the influence of culture on education and practice.

If that wasn't hard enough, the students terrified me. From a situation where Middle Eastern students treated you like a parent, drank in your every word and relied on you far too much, I had gone to a set up where the students questioned everything you said and didn't really need to come to class, because all they needed to know was on YouTube.

I am sure that I annoyed the hell out of the rest of the staff by my almost continuous recitation of, "In Bethlehem we did this" "Palestinian physios concentrate on this."

In the end a German colleague, not noted for his tact, told me in no uncertain terms "You are not in Bethlehem now. You are in Eastbourne. I don't want to hear either the "B" word or the "P" word again."

I think if the rest of my life had been better, I would not have felt so alone. I couldn't get used to having to choose which supermarket to go to, how to decide which cereal packet to buy and having five TV channels all speaking English. I realized that I was no longer in an Arab, Islamic-influenced culture when I saw how much flesh was on display as people walked down the street and how many TV programmes discussed sex so explicitly.

For a long time, I felt myself still reliving a past which was no longer anything more than the history of another person, but gradually began to feel at home in this country that was supposed to be my home and with this person who was now myself.

Nostalgia

There it sits on the windowsill, next to the CD player, a small photo album with photos from my days in the Middle East. This was the time before I had a digital camera, so they are "real" photos developed from negatives in a photographic shop, when you didn't know how they would turn out until you saw the pictures.

As I flick through, I see myself, looking very serious in gown and mortar board walking down the steps to graduation in the Great Hall at Bethlehem University. I glance at another photo of three of my "boys" fitting a chair they had made from cardboard for a small disabled boy in Jericho, while his father looks on hopefully. I smile as I peer at groups of students and remember the many occasions that had to be immortalized on film. The photo to which my eyes are drawn involves a group of students from 1989, most of whom are now respected senior professionals and proud parents and grandparents. This picture is special because two of those pictured are no longer alive. They share a name, Amjad and share the fact that they both died of heart attacks, although at different ages, times and places.

Amjad the younger, was a young man from Hebron who though visually impaired was one of the brightest stars in the class and invariably cheerful. We provided him with audio tapes of the set books and his prodigious memory meant that he could challenge me in class using what he remembered "reading". We didn't know that he had a weak heart as Palestinian students don't need a health check, so it was a shock to hear he had died in the bathroom at his home. I was privileged to attend one of the four days mourning at his parents' house and felt I had lost my own son.

Amjad the older, was a colleague from Gaza, who brought his whole family to live in Bethlehem. He was a gentle man, truly religious in faith and practice, with a slow smile and the ability to diffuse stress by telling feeble jokes. When political circumstances no longer permitted him to travel to Bethlehem, he moved back to Gaza, where he gained the reputation of being an elder statesman in his professional field. I visited Gaza a few times and during one such visit I stayed with him and his family. It was a joy to see him surrounded by his eight children and innumerable grandchildren. He had built a house for himself, his wife and those children still living at home. The plan had also been to build apartments for the two eldest sons and their families.

Unfortunately, they had run out of cement and because of the Israeli blockade, no more cement was allowed into Gaza. We heard he had experienced a number of heart attacks from which he recovered but that he could not be offered open heart surgery because of weak heart muscle.

Having received frantic texts and on Facebook Messenger from our graduates, I heard about the final attack from which he died. I remembered the last time I saw him tending the barbecue in his garden in Gaza, with his wife and surrounded by his children and grandchildren. The huge grin on his face indicated his pleasure and pride in them all as they took this fleeting opportunity to enjoy family life in the middle of tragedy.

When I heard the news of my friend's death, I felt great sadness for his wife and sympathy for his eldest son, who would now have to step into his father's very large shoes and take up the duties of family headship.

I glance again at the photos on the windowsill and remind myself that the passage of time has brought change to all those proudly smiling into the camera.

The Dream

I don't know when I started to have this dream, but it keeps coming back. And what is more everyone I meet has started to have it too. It came about this way. I was walking down a street towards the checkpoint. Normally I would not have done this as the closer I got the more I expected to be shot at. Today I took a chance because of the dream I had had the night before.

I couldn't believe it when the soldier instead of scowling at me and demanding I stop immediately, smiled and beckoned me forward. I didn't really believe him so approached warily. "Good afternoon my friend. How are you this fine day?"

I opened my mouth, but nothing came out except a cross between a cough and a giggle. "Fine, thank you. And yourself?" I managed to gasp. He took my hand and led me towards the turnstile where he pushed the gate to let me enter.

Inside the security office the border guard looked quite human and nodded his head as he asked for my identity card. Wordlessly I handed it to him. Well, I thought, maybe he had the same dream as me. Should I ask him? Maybe not, it might break the spell.

I began to walk down the main street and noticed that one of my neighbours was following me. "That was easier than usual" he sighed with relief. "I wonder why? Perhaps they had the same dream as me." I turned in amazement to him "You had it too?" I gasped. "What was your dream? How often have you had it?"

"It all started last week after I had been to collect my exit permission," he said.

On the way home I said to myself, "wouldn't it be great if people on both sides stopped hating each other, stopped fighting each other and treated each other as human beings instead of animals?" As I thought this, there was a momentary hush in the noise around me and a deep sigh that seemed to come from the centre of the earth.

I thought nothing more of it but that was the first night I had the dream. When I woke in the morning my wife said, "I had such a funny dream last night. I couldn't believe it. What I saw was beautiful but impossible."

I couldn't persuade her to tell me anything else, but I hugged my dream to me, and it made me feel happy all day. All that day I kept on meeting people who smiled at me, shook me by the hand but more importantly allowed me to go wherever I wanted in the city. Instead of suspicion, I encountered trust, instead of minimal words we had real conversations and instead of feeling depressed I felt joyful. Everything was fine as I went back through the check point at night, even though the soldiers had changed shift.

Next morning, I thought things would still be good and so approached the soldiers confidently. "Stop don't come any closer," they said. I looked around me and said to myself "what has changed?" Inside my head I heard a voice say, "yesterday was what could be possible." So why is today back to normal? Again. the voice came, "well we didn't think you were ready for such a big change yet."

We Said We Wouldn't Look Back

These words from a 1950s musical show express my concerns about returning to Palestine. I feel very strongly that one takes responsibility for the time that one is involved in a project but relinquishes that responsibility when the project finishes, or when one's part in it ends. When I left Bethlehem University in 1999, I vowed that I would not interfere in the running of the Physiotherapy Programme there. I would be grateful for the opportunity I had been given to contribute to physiotherapy education in Palestine and allow the local staff who took over the running of the programme to get on with it. I would not entertain ideas about, or listen to rumours, that standards might have gone down after I left.

I went back for the graduation of the last group of students I had taught, but after that it became difficult to go back because of the Second Intifada and my life became taken up with professional activities in the UK and elsewhere.

Returning to the UK meant teaching on a degree course in physiotherapy in a British university, a very different proposition from how I had left physiotherapy education in the UK in 1988. At that time physiotherapy education was at diploma level and hospital based. My learning curve during the first three months back in the UK was almost vertical as policies and procedures in UK universities were also very different from American-influenced universities in the Middle East. These concerns and the political situation in Palestine prevented an early return.

I finally went back to BU this January. My visit was not principally to see the graduates, but incidental to another task I had undertaken in Jerusalem. In the intervening 10+ years since returning to the UK, many graduates and colleagues had discovered me on Facebook and got in touch, asking me when I was coming back. My views on returning were also influenced by two BU graduates who came to the UK to do Masters' and

PhD level education. Their feeling was that there was still a role for me at BU.

The journey from Jerusalem to Bethlehem is fraught with difficulties as "the Wall" now separates the two places and the checkpoint into Bethlehem is very slow. I was advised to take the bus that circumvented the checkpoint as I was a foreigner and did not need permission to enter Jerusalem. I felt very guilty about this but was persuaded that the journey would be quicker, and I would be certain of arriving on time.

After many emails and phone calls between myself, the faculty at BU and the President of the Palestine Physiotherapy Association (PPTASS), it was finally agreed that I would conduct a half-day workshop on "Evidence-based Practice". I also did a similar workshop for the occupational therapists. Those who attended were a mixture of graduates, faculty members and senior students. It was very moving to see so many of our graduates now well respected professionally and especially, to see that the Heads of Physiotherapy and Occupational Therapy at the university were both people I had taught.

The approach of the workshop was interactive and low tech as I used a white board for summarizing discussion and afterwards made some hand-outs available. I emphasised that EBP involves using the best AVAILABLE evidence and we discussed what evidence was available in Palestine. This led into a discussion about the importance of understanding the clinical implications of research and engaging in the research process. There were some Palestinian physiotherapists present who had done higher studies, both locally and internationally. I was surprised to find that they had not offered, or been asked, to present the findings of their research at PPTASS meetings and encouraged them to do this.

The other key issue about EBP we discussed was if research crossed cultures. As much of the research in physiotherapy is based in the west, are the findings appropriate to practice in a Middle Eastern country such as Palestine?

We concluded that some aspects of physiotherapy, especially theory, was applicable across cultures, but many aspects of practice were heavily influenced by culture. These thoughts lead to a discussion about physiotherapy research already completed in Palestine and nearby Arab countries and its availability as evidence. The need for more local-based research and participants' own responsibility to bring this about was also considered.

It was a joy to facilitate discussion with such an open-minded group of participants and work with graduates themselves teaching students in both academic and clinical settings. I am glad that I did go back but am also glad that it was not immediately, but after some time.

Poem to my Students at Bethlehem University

I will put in a box the joy for life and learning,
you shared with me when you had nothing to be happy
about, except each new day that dawned.

I will put in a box the hospitality shared,
in refugee camps and remote villages sitting on the floor
eating with greasy hands, laughing, and drinking Coke.

I will put in a box the sadness of sons shot,
of fathers beaten, of daughters bereft and mothers weeping,
of homes destroyed and olive trees uprooted.

I will put in a box the sound of sirens,
of being half asleep in a sealed room.
watching scud missiles in dark starry skies.

I will put in a box my guilt at being able to leave,
and go home, to a safe place, a quiet house,
in a country without checkpoints or curfews.

This box is made of being called "terrorist",
being misunderstood, being occupied,
but its covers consist of patience and perseverance.

The Siege of Bethlehem

I had to remind myself to breathe – almost to remind my heart to beat but then I remembered that I had to remain silent if I wanted to evade capture. How did I get involved? Why did I go to the market that day? I knew exactly why – my mother sent me with food for my brother who is a member of Hamas. How this happened was a mystery to us all. One week he was a quiet young man studying business at university and the next he had wrapped a *kefiyah* round his face and strutted up and down the street with a rifle slung over his shoulder. He wouldn't tell us anything about his movements "because of security" he said.

The day it all became more personal was a Saturday and these boys had been baiting the young Israeli soldiers on the checkpoint. They tolerated this for a while and then marched into Bethlehem with their guns cocked. The chase led them up Hebron Road and then left at *Bab Isqaq*, past the deaf school and the Holy Family Hospital into the narrow streets of the *suk*. Playing cat and mouse with the soldiers, they made their way past the Lutheran Christmas Church and then down the steps past the Syrian Orthodox church.

All shops were sealed up and houses locked and bolted, all lights extinguished. The boys had the advantage over the soldiers as they had been born and raised in these streets, they also knew where they were making for, the Church of the Nativity in Manger Square, which had always looked more like a military building than a religious one. Despite the objections of the priests, they barricaded themselves in and began the long wait. After twenty-four hours the sounds of shooting had died down and my mother was concerned that my brother had no food. I must find a way to sneak into the church and take some to him. With a small backpack on and wearing my darkest clothes and my *kefiyah* hiding my face, I slid out of the back yard and crept down through the market.

I knew a back way in through the Armenian priests' living quarters that I assumed the Israelis were unaware of. I eased the door open slowly and prayed that it had been recently oiled. The last thing I needed was a creaking door to give me away. All went well and I eventually discovered my brother and his mates after creeping down the steps to the Nativity Grotto and hearing some sounds in the tunnel leading to St Jerome's Grotto. I tried the door and it opened whereupon I felt a hand over my face and a gun at my back. I was only released when Elias vouched for me.

After such a rough welcome I felt quite aggrieved, but my good humour was restored as they began to attack the food ravenously. Elias gave me messages for my mother and father and suggested I went back home via St Catherine's Catholic church. I was climbing the stairs to the church when I heard Hebrew being spoken in the courtyard, between me and freedom. Until now, this had been a great adventure but now it had become much more serious. I slid under one of the nearby pews and waited. The soldiers had obviously entered the church without permission and now I heard the priest telling them to leave. They were obviously reluctant to do so, and it was some minutes before they moved off, but to me it felt like an eternity.

Into the silence came the same voice, "you can come out now my son, they have gone." Emerging from behind the kneelers I saw Father Jean Manual, my English teacher from the Freres School. I gratefully made my way to the door as he placed his hand on my head, "go with God. Give my greetings to your father."

Another Manic Monday

Light was peeping through the blinds and Samira realised that a new day had begun, and she needed to be up and dressed, to be able to finish all the arrangements she had begun the previous day. Life was always like this on a Monday but even more so today. Her heart was heavy with thoughts about the future for her beloved eldest son. She would miss him so much.

Her mind listed all the tasks she must complete; bake fresh bread, make more *hummus and babaganoush*, make a salad and pick oranges from the tree by the back door. So much to do and so little time to do it. Fortunately, her two elder daughters were visiting with their children, they would help in the kitchen and the sounds of the children playing would soothe her bruised heart.

So much had been said and planned that brought her to this day and her mind went back to the numerous times the men of the family had sat around the table outside in the shade of the olive trees sipping tea, drinking *arak* and loudly discussing the future of her eldest son.

"I want my son to study medicine. That will give him a good start in life. It must be the best place we can afford."

"Of course, you do, *Abu Hanna*. But surely the best place is Damascus?"

"I have sent my son there to study law. He is doing well and is living with my cousin Farid."

"I have made up my mind that the Medical School in Istanbul is the best. That is where he will go."

That decision had brought them to this day when Hanna was leaving home, for how long, God only knew.

Samira remembered sitting with the other women, tears pricking her eyelids and a huge lump in her throat, listening to these men decide on the future of her beloved Hanna.

How could they understand a mother's anguish at the thought of her son being alone in a strange place? Who would cook for him, wash his clothes, and make sure he went to Mass every Sunday. Anything could happen to him. She shivered as she thought of all the temptations to a good Christian boy, in what was supposed to be a Muslim city but had the reputation of having all the evils of western culture.

However, she knew it was the custom that the men of the family, especially the father, made decisions about education and marriage in the family. *Abu Hanna's* word was law, after all he was paying for his children's education. She thought back to the times when young men had visited the house to be vetted as possible husbands for her daughters. She remembered how she felt when *Abu Hanna* had chosen a man from Mosul in Iraq for Amal, her eldest daughter and how they wept over each other the day the young couple left for their new home, knowing it would be months until they met again. Thank God that Rima had married a man in the next village, and they were able to see her every month, but who knew how long they would be close at hand as her husband had won a scholarship to Kiev in Ukraine.

Eventually all preparations were completed, and Hanna had managed to find a place for all the food his mother had pressed on him for the journey. His protests about not having enough room in his luggage and having more than enough to feed him all the way to Istanbul and back were of no avail. His mother's love had to be seen in tangible form. What would the neighbours think if she sent him off with less than this?

The whole family, mother, father, brothers and sisters, cousins and aunts and uncles plus a few close neighbours saw him off at the railway station, having been ferried in a convoy of taxis to Aleppo. So much kissing and hugging and weeping and hand wringing that Hanna couldn't bear it and prayed for the train to start. He did not realise then that this farewell would sustain his spirit in the dark first days of his time in Istanbul. At last, he climbed onto the train and closed the carriage door.

Opening the window, he leaned out to wave goodbye and kept on waving until his family were as small as specks of dust. Their last sight of him was a lone arm waving out of the window as the train gathered speed on its ten-hour journey to Istanbul.

Being Interviewed

I had been offered this job in Bethlehem, so I thought, by the people at Save the Children Fund in London. We had spent a whole morning discussing the political situation there, which extended over a very nice lunch in a restaurant in Holborn. I was under the impression that they had interviewed me. I began to see that, no, I was wrong.

"The Vice Chancellor of Bethlehem University wants you to go out there and see the situation for yourself."

This was during the First Intifada, the Palestinian uprising against Israeli occupation, when violence erupted daily between the Palestinian Shebab, the young men and the soldiers of the Israeli Defense Force. I had seen the infamous footage of a soldier striking an unarmed (unless you count stones) young Palestinian and breaking his leg.

"They don't want you to say you will accept the job here in the UK and then find you can't cope with the political situation there."

It sounded like a sensible idea.

So off I went and was escorted around East Jerusalem and Bethlehem by a Scandinavian social worker, coming to the end of her assignment with evident relief and an Irish American teacher on a short consultation visit who was very matter of fact about life in Bethlehem. The ten days I spent in their company gave me a clearer picture of what it would be like living there.

I did have meetings with some of the De La Salle Brothers who ran the university but didn't really meet any of the Palestinian staff as all Palestinian universities were closed by Israeli military order. It was explained to me that this new programme would go ahead at a place not yet named. It was considered vital that the young men being shot by Israeli soldiers needed up to date rehabilitation, not available locally.

However, I don't remember being interviewed, not

according to how I thought an interview should be done. I did not understand this low- key approach until much later when the Vice Chancellor and I interviewed a potential member of staff. When he finished his questions, he was surprised that I continued to ask what I wanted to know.

The night before I was to fly home, I was invited to supper at the Brothers community house, preceded by mass in their chapel. Being an Anglican I could more or less follow the service, what we would have called communion. About halfway through the service different individuals present voiced their petitions after which we all joined in with, "Lord in your mercy. Hear our prayer."

I suppose I was not listening very closely when I heard the Vice Chancellor say, "Lord we thank you that we have found the leader for the new physiotherapy programme," and I realised he was speaking about me. Instead of joining in the appropriate response I thought, 'Hang on a minute, don't bring God into it yet. I haven't made up my mind'.

I was in the middle of the situation before I knew I had begun. It seemed that my mind had been made up for me.

PHOTOGRAPHS

Page 54

Clinical supervision at Mount of David Orthopaedic Hospital, Bethlehem

First cohort of physiotherapy students, Bet Jala

Page 55

Physiotherapy upgraders paediatric workshop, Bethlehem

Physiotherapy upgraders workshop on mobilization techniques, Bethlehem

Page 56

Visiting Augusta Victoria Hospital, Jerusalem

A group of physiotherapy upgraders at graduation, Bethlehem

Page 57

Graduates workshop at Arab American University, Jenin

Working with children at Caritas Childrens Hospital, Bethlehem

Page 58

Visiting the Bethlehem Arab Society for Rehabilitation, Bet Jala

Teaching at Bethlehem University

Page 59

Physiotherapy graduates at Bethlehem University

Physiotherapy clinic, Bet Jala

Page 60

Physiotherapy colleagues in Gaza

Family barbecue in Gaza

Page 61

L'Arche workshop for disabled adults, Bethlehem

Church of Beatitudes, Galilee

Page 62

Check point in the Old City, Jerusalem

Beduin camp near Hebron

Page 117

View over Bethlehem and Bet Jala

Shepherds Fields, Bet Sahour

Page 118

Al Basma Centre for disabled adults, Bet Sahour

Children playing traditional musical instruments, Bethlehem

Page 119

Steps up to the roof, Hebron Old City

Page 120

The bells of the Church of the Nativity, Bethlehem

Donkey in an olive grove, near Bethlehem

Page 121

Mary Magdalene Russian Orthodox Church, Mount of Olives

Sunset over the sea in Gaza

Page 122

Inside the Church of the Holy Sepulchre, Jerusalem

Page 123

Mosaic in Jericho

Old City, Nablus

Page 124

Service at the baptismal Site, Jericho

Children performing traditional Palestinian dances, Bethlehem

Page 125

Inside the chapel at Bethlehem University

Page 126

Ethiopians Christians at the Week of Prayer for Christian Unity, Jerusalem

Rehabilitation workshop in Gaza

Page 127

Christmas in Manger Square, Bethlehem

ABOUT THE AUTHOR

Lesley lived and worked in the West Bank and Gaza Strip between 1988 and 1999. She headed up the team that developed and ran degree programmes in physiotherapy and occupational therapy at Bethlehem University and a short spell in Gaza at the UNRWA College of Nursing. As a result of these projects and an interest in Biblical sites, she travelled widely in Israel and the Occupied Palestinian Territories.

Since then, she has returned often to see friends, run workshops for graduates and support charities involved in working with children with disabilities, Christian communities and friendship projects with organisations and individuals.

Because of a continued interest in rehabilitation in Israel/Palestine it seems appropriate to donate all the revenue from sales of this book to an organization working with people with disability, Action around Bethlehem Children with Disability (ABCD).

BOURNE TO WRITE

Bourne to Write is an online creative writing workshop led by the writer, broadcaster and arts critic Roddy Phillips. The weekly Zoom workshops take a student-centred approach to creative writing, offering a range of strategies to help new writers develop their talent and skills. Writers are encouraged to explore their creative writing potential through self-awareness and self-discovery.

Bourne to Write workshops are suitable for aspiring writers of all levels and abilities and for anyone with a strong interest in reading and writing, who would like to deepen their understanding of the creative process. For more information on how you can join one of our workshops log onto...

bournetowrite.co.uk

How far is it to Bethlehem?

Printed in Great Britain
by Amazon

41288486R00118